"Of cour___ ___ ___ ___ dessert.___

When Dar___ g___ ___ ___ shocked look, Chase smiled. "The restaurant has three different kinds of cheesecake."

"What if cheesecake isn't what I had in mind?" she asked in her sexiest voice.

His brows went up. "Oh?"

"I may be more in the mood for ice cream," she said with a straight face.

"That sounds cold. Now, whipped cream—there are a lot of things you can do with whipped cream."

"You're naughty."

"That's what they say."

It wasn't what he'd said, but how he'd said it that threw her off balance. She couldn't keep going back and forth like this, engaging in foreplay, and not make a decision on how she wanted this night to end.

She tried to focus on the menu's entrées, but her thoughts immediately went back to the whipped cream. *Damn him.*

Blaze™

Dear Reader,

Talk about an idea that won't let go! About ten years ago I first heard about—get this—a job that pays you to exercise! And not even hard exercise like being a trainer. No, this job paid you to take hotel guests on interesting runs around New York City. Since my daily runs consisted of nothing but dirt roads and skipping over flagstones, I figured I deserved to be paid for it. Can you imagine running through beautiful Central Park or in and around all those fabulous old buildings in Manhattan? I can, and did, in *All or Nothing*.

My heroine Dana McGuire has turned her passion for fitness and her love of the city into a job that not only pays well, but lets her meet all kinds of interesting people. None, however, compare to Chase Culver, a mysterious, gorgeous man from Texas who gets her heart beating double time even before the first step. Together they get all the exercise they'll ever need, and not from running.

I hope you'll get a healthy heart workout yourself as you jump into their adventure.

Happy reading!

Debbi

ALL OR NOTHING
Debbi Rawlins

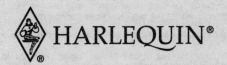

HARLEQUIN®

TORONTO • NEW YORK • LONDON
AMSTERDAM • PARIS • SYDNEY • HAMBURG
STOCKHOLM • ATHENS • TOKYO • MILAN • MADRID
PRAGUE • WARSAW • BUDAPEST • AUCKLAND

ISBN-13: 978-0-373-79421-8
ISBN-10:   0-373-79421-5

ALL OR NOTHING

www.eHarlequin.com

Printed in U.S.A.

ABOUT THE AUTHOR

Debbi Rawlins lives in central Utah, out in the country, surrounded by woods and deer and wild turkeys. It's quite a change for a city girl, who didn't even know where the state of Utah was until several years ago. Of course, unfamiliarity never stopped her. Between her junior and senior years of college she spontaneously left home in Hawaii, and bummed around Europe for five weeks by herself. And much to her parents' delight, returned home with only a quarter in her wallet.

Books by Debbi Rawlins

HARLEQUIN BLAZE

 *Men To Do
**Do Not Disturb
†Million Dollar Secrets

This is for the ladies at Eureka Bingo in Mesquite.
With special thanks to Donna, Wilma,
Betty and Lin-duh.
Thanks for always entertaining me and helping me
wind down between books. You guys are terrific.

1

IGNORING the annoying catcalls from one of the hard hats inspecting a pothole on Fifth Avenue, Dana McGuire stopped at the intersection and stretched out her calf muscles while she waited for the light to change. In true Manhattan tradition, the other pedestrians, dressed mostly in business suits, swirled around her, crossing against the light and prompting some angry horn-honking in spite of the police cruiser that swung onto Fifty-seventh Street.

Five years now she'd lived in the city, and it hadn't changed one tiny bit. She had. No choice there. Survival of the fittest. She straightened. Hmm. Not a bad name for her new fitness club. Go figure. She'd spent weeks trying to come up with a name before she applied for a license, and there it was. Not that she had all of the start-up money yet. But she was almost there. Six months and she'd be ordering equipment and signing the lease.

The walk signal flashed and she jogged across the street to the mailbox in front of the St. Martine Hotel, where she had a client this morning, and deposited her bimonthly letter to her parents. E-mail would be so much easier, but they didn't own a computer and she doubted they ever would. Third-generation farmers, who'd only recently splurged on a satellite dish for their ten-year-old television, neither of her parents had ridden on an airplane or seen the ocean. In fact, they hadn't stepped foot out of Indiana.

Lucky for her, since she didn't have to worry about any surprise visits from them. Not that she didn't love them both to pieces, but they thought she was someone she wasn't and she didn't have the heart to set them straight.

"Morning, Dana." St. Martine's veteran doorman with his watery blue eyes and pleasant round face held open the lobby door for her.

"Thanks, George. Looks like it's gonna be another scorcher," she said, pulling her ponytail tighter so that the hair stayed off the back of her neck. Her hair was too long and totally impractical, especially for running every day. If she had an ounce of sense she'd whack it all off. But vanity won out every time she tried to talk herself into it, which really ticked her off.

She wasn't Borden County's reigning Miss Teen Dairy anymore, nor had she participated in a beauty pageant for the past six years. Or ever would again. But the long blond mane had earned her at least one commercial hawking shampoo, and even then, she'd shared the spotlight with a brunette and a redhead. A far cry from taking Broadway by storm.

"You think it's hot out here," George whispered, and nodded his head toward the lobby. "Heard there was another one last night."

"Oh, no. What did they get?"

"No one's saying. We've all been warned to keep mum. Junior's threatening to write up any employee caught discussing the theft." George's ruddy face lit with a grin. "You didn't hear a peep from me," he said, winking and stepping back to let her into the lobby.

"Not a word," Dana agreed, smiling.

Everyone knew George referred to the new assistant manager as Junior. A recent Cornell graduate, Kyle Williams would rid the hotel of any employee over forty if he had his way, but the unions were too strong and George wasn't about to give up his six-figure job opening doors for the hotel's wealthy guests.

Heck, Dana wouldn't mind getting in on that kind of action herself, but there were literally waiting lists for those types of jobs all over the city. Although, as it was, she did like her job. She was her own boss and got paid to exercise, which she did every day anyway. Amazing what an out-of-towner was willing to pay to be escorted on a run through Central Park or along the Hudson River.

The lobby was more subdued than usual. One of the housekeeping staff, who had to be new because Dana didn't recognize her, dusted around the large vase of fresh-cut flowers sitting on the Asian-inspired table that served as the lobby's centerpiece. A couple in business suits stood talking near the elevators and another guest leaning on the black-lacquered front desk appeared to be checking in, or, given the early hour, perhaps checking out.

Dana's friend Amy was one of the clerks working behind the desk, but she wasn't the one helping the man and, after meeting Dana's eyes, she walked purposely to the far end of the counter. Dana got the message and met her near the concierge's unmanned smoky-glass cubicle. Odd. Kelly was always there. The three of them usually grabbed a ten-minute cup of coffee before Dana met up with her first client.

"Where is she?" she asked, getting a bad vibe from the way Amy's anxious gaze scanned the lobby.

"Security." Amy's voice was low. "We had another theft last night. Fourth one this month."

"So why are they talking to Kelly?"

"They're talking to everybody. I wouldn't be surprised if they asked to see you."

"Me?"

Amy nodded, her large dark eyes coming back to Dana. "Nothing personal. It's just that you've practically been a fixture here the past couple of months."

"Thanks to all the business you guys throw me." She glanced over her shoulder, unnerved that she'd be of any interest to security. "I still don't understand why they'd want to talk to me though."

"You were on the property yesterday. That makes you a candidate for questioning." Amy gave her a wicked smile. "But then again, Kyle probably would protect you."

Dana rolled her eyes. The assistant manager had been a pain in the ass from the first day she'd met him. He'd asked her out three times in three weeks. She'd been polite in her first two refusals, not so subtle the last time. If he tried one more time, she wouldn't be responsible for her actions.

"Hey, guys." Kelly joined them, already slipping off her navy blue blazer as she rounded her desk. "I'm afraid I won't have time for coffee."

"How was it?" Amy asked. "You weren't gone long."

"Pretty straightforward." Kelly pushed long slender fingers through her strawberry-blond hair and then lowered herself onto her chair, her gaze going to her calendar.

Like Dana and Amy and countless others, she'd come to New York from a small midwestern town hoping to make it big. Like them, she'd failed miserably, although landing the assistant concierge job had been quite a coup. Good money. A certain amount of prestige. And it beat waiting tables like some of the less-fortunate hopefuls they'd met in the early days at casting calls and standing in line at the unemployment office.

Amy glanced over her shoulder and then leaned closer. "What kind of questions did they ask?"

"They just want to confirm shift times, if and when you left your station, that sort of thing."

Dana checked her watch. Five minutes until her appointment with Chase Culver. After that she had to hurry across town to meet her regular Tuesday-morning client. She wouldn't have time to talk to anyone today. Not that she had anything to say. "What was taken?"

Behind her someone noisily cleared their throat. Without looking she knew who it was by the way dread crawled over her skin.

"Talking about the theft, are we, ladies?"

She turned to Kyle with wide-eyed innocence, and in a loud voice said, "There was another theft? Here? When?"

He gave her a wry look before adjusting his left cuff link and sliding an exasperated look toward the front desk. The guest checking out turned toward them with interest.

Good thing Dana couldn't see Kelly and Amy's faces—it would've been hard to keep a straight one herself. Singing had once been her claim to fame, not acting. Although she'd taken enough classes when she'd first arrived in the city.

"I'd appreciate you keeping your voice down, Dana," Kyle said in that proper-Bostonian tone that was as phony as his knockoff Rolex. "We don't need our guests alarmed."

She smiled. "No, that wouldn't be good for business." She backed away, throwing a look at Kelly and Amy. "See you guys later."

"I didn't mean to chase you off," Kyle said with that creepy smile of his, while putting his hand on her arm.

She did all she could not to jerk away. Instead she kept backing up until contact was naturally broken. "I have to meet a client."

He let his smarmy gaze wander down the front of her tank top, down her Spandex running shorts to her bare legs. "Of course."

She couldn't stand to look at him another second and abruptly turned toward the house phone by the elevator. The doors opened and a tall, wiry man in his early thirties walked out. He had dark longish hair, piercing blue eyes, and he wore shorts and a T-shirt hugging really broad shoulders. Holy cow, it wasn't Christmas and she hadn't been particularly good all year, but please, please be Chase Culver.

CHASE KNEW it was her. Not because he'd done his homework on her last night. Nothing on a piece of paper could prepare him for Dana McGuire in the flesh. Tall, slim and blond, her sapphire-blue eyes were enough to take the wind out of him. Centerfold material. This was the kind of woman men made fools of themselves over. Lost marriages and fortunes and reputations. Good to remember that.

"Dana?"

She smiled. "How did you know?"

"We're the only two people underdressed."

"Oh, right." She gave a small sheepish shrug as she glanced down at her shorts.

He jumped on the opportunity to take another look himself. Long perfect legs that stopped just this side of heaven. Keeping his mind on business wasn't going to be easy. In fact, he needed to revamp his bio quickly. The phony businessman-from-Houston spiel he'd prepared was okay, but to get the most bang for his buck, he had to bump it up. Become the kind of man she needed most. Because basically there were two reasons why a woman who looked like her came to New York, and he'd bet his '67 Mustang convertible he knew what had lured her to the bright lights.

"Have you already done some stretching?" she asked, leading him toward the lobby doors.

They passed near the front desk where two women in hotel uniforms openly stared. The guy in the suit was one of those prissy twerps that grated on Chase. "Some."

"Do you jog regularly?" Her gaze briefly caught on his ringless left hand, and then ran down his body.

His gut tightened when he saw more than professional curiosity darken her eyes. This assignment was gonna be a bitch. "Maybe three times a week. I'm usually too busy for anything more."

"How many miles were you thinking we should go today?"

"Five."

Her eyebrows went up.

"Or seven."

She stopped short of the doors, a hint of a smile on her lips. "How many do you usually run?"

"Well, darlin', that depends on who's chasing me."

She gave a small shake of her head. "I'll take that as seven."

He exhaled slowly. His friggin' ego had gotten him into enough trouble. "Five is good."

"Central Park okay with you?"

There had to be a better way than running in this heat to get to know her, ask her a few questions without sounding suspicious. Too bad he hadn't come up with one. "Fine."

"Okay." She pushed through the doors and they'd barely hit the sidewalk when she started them on a brisk walk. Pedestrian traffic wasn't too bad and in a matter of minutes they could see the park. "How long have you been doing this?" he asked as they waited at the light across from the park entrance where a line of horses and carriages waited for the tourists.

"About three years." She hadn't stopped moving, but continued to walk in place and shake out her arms. She got more than a few second looks and not because of anything she did. No makeup and her hair plastered back, she was still stunning.

He wondered if Roscoe had told him everything. If that ol' boy had slept with her and left that part out, Chase was gonna wring his neck. He eyed her again, trying not to be too obvious. Nah, she wouldn't hook up with an old windbag like Roscoe. Even if the guy was rich. But then what the hell did Chase really know about her? "Are you from New York?"

"Indiana."

"What brought you here to the big city?" he asked causally.

Her smile was brief and sad, but wasn't going to stop him from lying through his teeth.

The light turned green, and she entered the crosswalk without answering him. She checked her watch. "You set the pace, but I'll make sure we're back in time for you to get to your eleven-thirty meeting. Ready?"

"Let's go."

For the first mile she was quiet except to warn him when a turn was coming up. They ran at a faster clip than he'd anticipated and he needed to get a conversation going while he could still run, breathe and talk at the same time. A year back he'd been in great shape and this would've been no sweat, but now not so much. The last twelve months had been the year from hell. Too much shit had gone down, none of it that he could control.

"You have a lot of clients?" He slowed down, pretending to watch a kid throw breadcrumbs to the ducks clustered at the edge of a small man-made lake.

She immediately downshifted. "Enough."

"A woman of few words. Or can't you keep up the pace and talk?"

She slid him an amused look. "I'm a personal trainer when I'm not doing this."

"You work in a club?"

"No, I go to people's homes."

Interesting. He made a mental note to check into it. That kind of history could work in her favor. Or put a nail in her coffin. "Must pay pretty well. This city ain't cheap."

She laughed softly. "Think about how much you're paying me to babysit you for an hour."

"Good point."

"How are you doing?"

"Still breathing."

"We've gone almost three miles. After this next curve we'll head back to the hotel via the east side of the park." She wasn't breathing hard, and unlike him, hadn't even broken a sweat.

"I'm glad you know where you're going. I'm totally lost."

"That's what keeps me in business."

Chase grunted. That was about all he could manage at the moment. The three miles weren't as much the problem as the pace he'd initially set. He should've taken it easier. Hell, his wound was still tender because he hadn't allowed it to heal properly. If only he had a brain the size of his ego.

A group of chatty young kids obviously on a field trip crossed their path and slowed them down. He wasn't complaining. He wanted to shake each of their grimy little hands. Once the way was clear again, Dana shot him a questioning look. He stuck to a slow jog and she stayed beside him.

"I didn't realize it was so humid here," he said. "Nothing

like Houston, mind you, where the air is thicker than my mama's country gravy."

"That's where you're from?"

He nodded. "I just bought a house near Hollywood so I've been kind of bouncing back and forth."

She checked her watch again. "We're going to have to pick it up a bit to get you back in time."

Damn it, he'd baited the hook and she hadn't even taken a nip. "Ever been to California?"

"Nope. I haven't been farther west than Indiana."

"The west coast is like living in a whole different country. Haven't decided if I like it or not yet." He let a few moments lapse and when it was obvious she wasn't going to comment, he added, "But that's where the talent is, they tell me. Of course I'm thinking I might find a mother lode here on Broadway."

She slowly looked at him, her brows furrowed with curiosity. "What kind of business are you in?" She blushed. "If you don't mind my asking."

"Up until now I've been involved in oil mostly. That's how my daddy made the family money, anyway." He paused and grinned. "I'm what you call going to divest and spend some of that money on films."

She took a moment to digest what he'd said, and he was pleased to see interest flicker across her face. "You're a producer."

"That's right. I have my eye on a play that I think will turn into a nice box-office hit. I'm meeting with the playwright tomorrow."

"Ah." She played it cool, scarcely showing anymore reaction, but he knew he'd gotten her attention.

"Wish I could tell you which one, darlin', but I'm a bit superstitious about these things."

"No, I don't blame you. I didn't mean to be nosy."

He winked. "I thought we were just having a friendly conversation."

She didn't smile. "It's just another mile out of the park. Want to pick up the pace for the last stretch?"

"Okay," he said, wishing he knew what was going on in that pretty head of hers. What was her story? Had she come to New York to act? Model? Find a rich husband? He'd bet she was more ambitious than that. But places like New York and Hollywood could be ruthless and unforgiving and shatter a young girl's dreams into a million pieces. Cause a lot of heartache and disappointment. Enough to make a person bitter. And bitterness changed a person.

The small ranching town outside of Dallas where he'd grown up had produced a couple of Hollywood hopefuls. Ashley Morgan had won most of the beauty pageants from Dallas to the panhandle, twirling that baton of hers and easing out everyone in the talent category. Senior year he'd gone out with her twice, probably due to curiosity on her part because of his muddy reputation, but he didn't have anything she needed to further her career, so it had ended pronto. Hadn't bothered him none.

Nah, ol' Ashley hadn't been the sharpest tool in the shed, but she had a body that wouldn't quit. He'd heard it had gotten her a bit part in a B movie, then she got married to a fat, rich oilman and had a whole passel of kids.

They jogged around a curve and he saw the lineup of horses and carriages, and knew he had only a few minutes of information-gathering left. They had another appointment tomorrow morning, but he didn't want to wait that long to find out what made Dana McGuire tick.

"I know I'm not the first one to tell you that you have

perfect bone structure. You ever do any modeling? Is that why you came to New York?"

She hesitated, long enough that he expected her to tell him to go to hell. Great. The last thing he needed was her clamming up. He'd gone too fast, come on too strong. He should've waited until tomorrow to get to the next level, but he'd acted like a damn rookie. Which he wasn't. He knew better. This was too important to screw up. If she had the ring, he needed to get it back.

2

"I WANTED to sing," Dana said finally. "Or act. That's why I came to New York. I was hoping to find work." She shrugged. "It didn't pan out, but I found something else I like to do. Something I like better." She'd told herself that often enough that it should be true by now. To some degree it was.

Fitness had always been important to her. She'd run track in high school, and when she'd traveled the pageant circuit back in her teens, she'd used the stage to push fitness as a higher priority in schools. She'd always been passionate about the need to stay active as a health issue, but if she were given the chance at a singing or acting career…

No, she could not go there. After struggling for four years, and lying to her family back home, she'd made peace with her life. It was a good life, too. She had great friends, a family who loved her, a business that had grown impressively over the past three years. One that was a lot kinder than the entertainment industry. She was happy. Content.

"A singer, huh? Now, that surprises me."

"Why?" They'd hit the street and she was suddenly anxious to get him back to the hotel and end their conversation. No use stirring up old hurts. So what if he was here scouting talent? She'd learned the hard way that she wasn't anything special. Just a small-town girl who'd once stood a foot above the rest. Her hopes had died long ago. There were hundreds of women hungrier and more talented than she. Let him go use his urban-cowboy charm on one of them.

"Just figured that—well, guess it doesn't matter."

Fine with her. "There's the hotel," she said abruptly and pointed. "See it?"

"Yep." He stopped, his gaze narrowing, a smile playing at the corners of his mouth. "You giving me the brush off?"

To avoid getting run over by a group of Japanese tourists, she was forced to move back against a building. "Do you mind? My other appointment is across town."

The large group was too busy listening to their guide and crowded the sidewalk to the point that Chase was literally pushed up against her. He flattened his hand against the brick beside her head and braced himself to keep from crushing her breasts.

"Sorry," he murmured, his musky scent of pine and sweat oddly pleasing.

She had a feeling he wasn't one bit sorry judging by the way his gaze stayed fixed on her mouth. "No problem."

"Hope I didn't hurt you." He was a good four inches taller than her, and she was no slouch at five-nine.

She smiled. "They're gone."

"What?"

"You can move back now."

He swung his gaze toward the retreating group. "Ah." And then he straightened and lowered his hand, his eyes coming back to her face, his mouth curving in a sly grin. "Who knew you could get stampeded in New York City?"

She sidestepped him and moved closer to the street where she could get some much-needed air. "I'm sorry, but I'm going to be late."

"What about your payment?"

"Are we still on for tomorrow morning?"

"Most definitely. I believe I booked you for a third morning, as well?"

"Right." She stuck her hand out to hail a cab even though she really had plenty of time to hoof it the nine blocks to her next appointment. Best she get away from him now. Tomorrow she'd be better composed. "We'll settle up at the end of your stay."

"Why, you're mighty trusting."

A cab pulled to the curb and she opened the door. "Yeah." Too trusting. Stupidly naive, in fact. As a result, she'd made mistakes. Shameful ones she could barely stand to think about. "Must be my midwest upbringing," she murmured as she slid into the safety of the cab. God, when was she ever going to learn?

AFTER EATING a late lunch in the hotel's bistro-style restaurant, which to Chase meant small portions, large tab, he stopped at the front desk. He recognized the short, dark-haired front-desk clerk from this morning when he'd met Dana in the lobby.

He also recognized the name on the gold tag she wore. She was on his list. "Good afternoon, Amy."

She smiled, looking prettier than at first glance. "Good afternoon, Mr. Culver. What can I do for you?"

For a moment, it took him aback that she knew his name. But this was one of those ritzy hotels that pampered guests with big fluffy bath towels and Godiva chocolates on the pillows, so maybe it wasn't that odd. He'd never stayed in a place like this before. Doubted he ever would again unless he was on the job.

"Well, darlin', you can tell me if you have a big safe in the back for me to keep some of my valuables." He gave her one of the big smiles that had gotten him into the back rooms of high-stakes' poker games and into more trouble than he cared to think about.

"Yes, of course." She smiled back. "But you do know you have a private one in your room, as well?"

"Yes, ma'am." He glanced over at the bellman standing at the end of the counter, and then Chase lowered his voice, "But I've heard rumors about a couple of thefts here in the past month."

Amy blinked. "Um…"

"Now, I'm sure you've been instructed not to talk about it," he said, leaning part way across the desk so that their faces were only inches apart. "And I don't wanna get you in any trouble, but you see, I have this expensive diamond necklace I just purchased and I would be real unhappy if anything happened to it."

She glanced around, opened her mouth to speak and then promptly shut it again. Their eyes met and she briefly pursed her lips. "If you'd like us to keep something in the hotel safe, that certainly can be arranged."

Damn. He must be losing his touch. "But you think my room safe is sufficient?"

Her gaze narrowed and she bit indecisively at her lower lip. "I don't have an opinion in that regard," she said finally.

Chase smiled, wondering how hard he should push. "I'll think on it." He pushed away from the counter, at the same time noticing that no one manned the concierge desk. "Do you know when the concierge will be back?"

"I'll page Kelly right away."

Perfect. She was the assistant and just the woman he wanted to speak with. "No hurry," he said. "Just looking for restaurant reservations. I'll come back in an hour."

He felt Amy's gaze on him until he rounded the corner where he ended up near the double doors to the Crystal Ballroom. A member of the housekeeping staff was polishing an ornate brass lamp that sat on a table near the sign for the restrooms. She barely looked up and no one else was in sight so he pulled out the small notebook he kept in his inside breast pocket.

When his finger caught on something he looked down and realized he hadn't yet removed the price tag from the new navy blue blazer he'd bought yesterday before getting on the plane to New York. He muttered a curse, glanced around to make sure no one had sneaked up on him, and then ripped out the tag.

He only owned one suit, which, unfortunately, had seen more funerals than weddings. His other sports jacket had gotten him through dozens of court appearances, but was slightly too worn for his role as Chase Culver, rich producer, son of an oilman. The snakeskin boots he wore he'd gladly forked over five hundred bucks for two years ago. There were some things a man just didn't scrimp on.

After flipping through a couple of pages of his notebook, he found the name of the St. Martine's head of security. Gil Wagoner was an ex-cop who had retired after twenty-one years on the job. Chase hadn't managed to pull his jacket, but he did know that the man's record hadn't been particularly remarkable. Not a bad thing. Maybe no commendations decorated his walls, but he hadn't been brought up on any charges, either. Probably one of those guys who showed up every day to eventually get that pension. No crime in that. A warm body in a uniform was all that was needed sometimes.

Chase exhaled and thought for a minute. He wasn't quite ready to talk to the man yet. Better to get his own feel first.

Let his gut point him in a direction before finding out who security or the cops thought looked good for the theft. They had to figure it was an inside job. Roscoe hadn't been the only one who'd been ripped off. Chase knew of at least one other theft. Who knew how many more the hotel was keeping under wraps? No matter. Two was enough to make him think the perp was right here. Not another guest, but an employee.

Or someone like Dana.

Man, he hoped not. But she had means and opportunity and maybe a motive he didn't know about yet, so he couldn't rule her out. Wouldn't be the first time a pretty face and great body had waylaid an investigation.

His cell phone rang, snagging the attention of the young woman polishing the lamp. He checked the caller ID and decided to let Buddy leave a message. Whatever his ex-partner had to say would be better discussed in the privacy of Chase's room. He flipped the cell shut, briefly catching the eye of the maid. She smiled shyly and quickly looked away.

Chase tucked the small notebook and phone back into his pocket. Then he adjusted his collar and put his game face on. No use passing up an opportunity. The young woman slid him another look. He smiled and moved toward her. "Good morning, ma'am."

WHEN Dana entered the lobby the next morning, Amy was busy helping a guest. Kelly was on the phone. Dana checked her watch. She still had fifteen minutes before she had to meet Chase and she'd hoped the girls could get away for a cup of coffee.

She really wanted to tell them about him. Naturally she wasn't interested in his projects or what kind of talent he was scouting, but like her, Kelly and Amy had both come from small midwestern towns looking to break into show business. Unlike her, they hadn't given up.

Kelly hung up the phone and motioned Dana over to her desk. "You have time for coffee?" Kelly asked, shooting a look toward the door to the executive offices.

"Absolutely. I purposely came early."

"You have a client?" Kelly closed her appointment book and slipped her gold Cross pen into the top drawer of her black-lacquer-and-glass desk.

"Yep."

"Same one as yesterday?"

Dana nodded. "Chase Culver. He's the reason I wanted to talk to the two of you."

"I'd like to do more than talk to him. The guy's hot."

She shrugged. "He's okay."

Kelly snorted. "Are we talking about the same man?"

Dana grinned. "So he's a little more than okay."

Kelly rolled her eyes and started to walk away.

"What about Amy?" Dana glanced over at their friend who looked more subdued than usual.

"She can't take a break yet. She's spent the last hour in the security office. Brenda is there now so there's no one to cover for her."

"An hour?" Dana fell into step beside Kelly as they passed the elevators and headed for the door that would lead them to what the employees affectionately called the dungeon, officially known as the back-of-the-house, where the cafeteria, housekeeping and lockers were located.

Technically, Dana wasn't supposed to go back there since she wasn't an employee, but no one had ever said a word and since the other two couldn't leave the property for their breaks they'd always grabbed a quick cup of coffee in the cafeteria.

"Everyone who worked during the thefts has been scheduled to meet with security," Kelly explained. "It's a pain in the ass, but I can see management's point."

"I get that, but Amy was there for an hour?"

"I haven't gotten the scoop from her yet." Kelly entered the cafeteria first and went straight for the coffee station. She nodded to one of the engineers who looked up from the newspaper he was reading. "I heard that one of the room service waiters was questioned for nearly two hours."

"Well, those guys are actually on the guest floors all the time so I can see why." Dana poured herself half a cup, leaving out the cream and sugar. That was all she allowed herself before running. "Even if they aren't suspects they might've seen something helpful."

"Yeah, I suppose." Kelly chose a secluded table in the corner, although only a few other people were taking their breaks. She took a hasty sip, muttered a curse and jerked away from the steaming cup. She exhaled sharply. "But Amy hardly ever goes up on the guest floors."

Dana had taken the seat opposite her and faced the doorway. If Kyle showed up she was out of here. The man could hurt her business so she'd kept her mouth shut, but she wasn't going to stick around and take any harassment. She looked at Kelly and noticed the strain around her mouth and eyes. "Are you worried about Amy?"

Kelly's eyebrows lifted in surprise. She blinked and then waved a dismissive hand. "No. I got this letter from my mom…" Kelly rubbed her temples.

"Oh, that." Dana's light remark belied the sympathy that ran deep. Being disappointed in yourself was one thing, but letting everyone back home know what a failure you'd become…well that was hard to stomach. It didn't help to keep up the lie. Contact with old friends and family just kept getting harder, more complicated, until you didn't know which end was up. "I might have some good news."

"Yeah?" Kelly braved another sip, a curious lack of interest in her face. "I could use some good news."

Dana spotted Amy at the door of the cafeteria. "Amy's here."

"Good. I'd like to hear what security said to her."

Their friend joined them at the table and the conversation immediately focused on her meeting with security.

"Man, those guys aren't kidding." Amy shook her head at Dana's offer to get her coffee. "Daryl kept firing questions at me like I was some kind of criminal."

Kelly frowned. "Didn't he just ask you to go to the movies with him last week?"

"Yeah, the stupid jerk wanted me to go see one of those juvenile comedies. As if."

Dana knew the security guard, but only by reputation. "Maybe he's giving you a hard time because you turned him down."

"No, I heard they're coming down hard on everyone." Kelly shook her head. "Still, they have no reason to be suspicious of the front-desk people."

Amy sighed. "Except I made several housekeeping requests on the nights of two of the thefts. Apparently one of the guests involved denied calling the front desk for extra pillows and I was the one who'd logged the request."

"So?" Dana didn't get it. "You wouldn't have been the one to take the pillows to the guest floor."

Amy's expression turned grim. "After the housekeeping runner goes home at eleven, depending on who's available, either the supervisor or a desk person fills guests' requests."

Dana sank back in her chair. "And tag, you were it."

"That's what they say. I don't remember." Amy growled with frustration. "I only work two lousy nights a week. Why did the thefts have to happen during my shift?"

Kelly briefly touched her hand. "Ah, sweetie, don't worry about it. Let them make their reports. They're just doing their job. Nothing will come of this."

"Still, it's humiliating."

Kelly looked at Dana. "Let's talk about something more pleasant. You have good news for us?"

She checked her watch. Not much time. "Turns out my client is a producer. He's here to meet with a playwright for a film he's backing. He didn't say it in so many words, but he might be looking for local talent that can take on the big screen."

"Chase Culver?" Amy asked, and at the same time Kelly said, "The hottie?"

"Yeah."

"He's a producer?" Amy shook her head. "He doesn't look like a producer. The guy's yanking your chain."

Kelly nodded. "I'm with Amy on that one. He's a little on the rough side, don't you think?"

"The family money comes from oil. He's decided to dabble in the movie business."

"Hmm." Kelly chuckled. "Expensive way to get laid."

"I don't think it's like that," Dana said, surprised at her defensiveness. "I mean, the guy could walk into any Manhattan bar and find someone to help him pull off his boots."

"True." Amy glanced conspiratorially at Kelly.

"What?" Dana got defensive again. "I'm not interested, if that's what you're implying."

Kelly laughed. "If you've got a pulse, you're interested in the man."

Dana pushed back from the table. "Here I thought I was doing you guys a favor."

Kelly finished her coffee, her obvious indifference not quite computing. Of the three of them she was the most diversely talented, able to sing, act and dance. She'd also been the most ambitious, keeping up on every casting call and arranging her days off accordingly. "How?"

"Look, I don't know what kind of film he's looking at producing, but why not throw your hats into the ring? It's not as if we haven't all stood in line for hours and hours for a two-minute audition just to get thrown out on our rears."

Oddly, it was Amy who seemed more excited. "Is he holding auditions?"

"Not yet. Not that I know of, anyway. He seems to be in the scouting stage." Troubled by her attitude, Dana stared at Kelly. "I thought you'd be all over this opportunity."

Kelly sighed. "I'm tired. This town is finally getting to me."

Amy's mouth dropped open. She briefly looked over at Dana, who understood the disbelief in Amy's face. "You? Miss Insanely Optimistic? You're giving up?"

"I think eight years of heartache is enough." Kelly drove a frustrated hand through her curly hair. "I've got to get back to work." She hesitated. "Look, I was going to wait and tell you guys once I made up my mind for sure, but my mom told me there's an opening for an assistant manager at the local bank back home. The manager is an old family friend and the job is pretty much mine if I want it."

"Shut up!" Amy's face went pale.

Dana knew she didn't look so hot herself. How could this be? Not gung-ho Kelly. She never ever lost hope. Anyone would've bet she'd be the last woman standing. "You're going back to Wisconsin?"

Kelly shrugged. "The cost of living is lower and I might as well use my business degree…" She smiled sadly. "As much as it pains me to admit it, I'm going to be thirty next month."

"Thirty?" Amy frowned. "That's right. Wow."

Kelly gave her a wry look. "I've got to face facts. Thirty is way too old for this town."

"What about that new guy you've been seeing?" Dana asked when she found her voice again. She hated the thought of Kelly leaving. Foolishly, the idea had never occurred to her that their threesome would ever be broken up, and the concept was hard to grasp. "Is it over already?"

"No. Everything is good." Kelly stood. "Look, I shouldn't have brought this up yet. Miranda won't be back from vacation for another two weeks and so obviously I wouldn't give notice yet. And then again, I haven't made a decision. I really have to get back to work before Kyle gets in my face."

"But what about this guy Culver?" Amy got up, too, so abruptly she nearly knocked her chair over. "Don't you want to know what that's about?"

The two other employees remaining in the cafeteria looked up with avid interest. Kelly lowered her voice. "Maybe. But I've got to give the bank my answer soon. You guys break a leg." She winked, and left without waiting for Amy or Dana.

Amy shook her head, still looking stunned. "That was scary."

"Yeah." Dana was feeling pretty shaken herself. She got rid of her unfinished coffee, afraid to look at her watch. She had to be late, but she couldn't seem to make herself move toward the door. "Did you see this coming at all?"

"Hell, no."

"Me neither."

"Yeah." Amy smoothed back her dark hair. "Wow. I'd like to go slam back a couple of shots, but I have to get back to the desk."

Dana sighed, and walking side by side, they headed for the door. "I've got to meet Chase."

Amy's chin came up. "You think he's legit?"

She shrugged. "I don't have any reason not to."

"You going for it?"

Dana swallowed. "I haven't auditioned in three years."

"So?"

"So, I like what I'm doing."

Amy snorted. "Right."

What Dana should've pointed out was that she'd quit three years ago. Moved on. No more pie-in-the-sky dreams for her. She had no business nurturing even the teensiest hope. Yet here she was, holding her breath.

3

CHASE BENT over to pull on his sweat socks, wincing with the effort. Yesterday's run—his first with Dana—hadn't tested his physical endurance as much as the hundred sit-ups he'd foolishly punished himself with last night. An equal amount of push-ups hadn't fazed him, but then again, the recent double bullet wound near his ribs had made crunches a bitch.

He promised himself that tonight he was taking it easy. Just him and that king-size bed. Throw in some room service and the television remote, he'd be all set. And if Dana were to...

Shit. What the hell was wrong with him? He couldn't be thinking like that. Yeah, she had legs that could wrap nicely around a man's waist and a high firm backside that you could set a beer on, but she was still a possible suspect. Just like the rest of the people on his list. So he'd better remember to keep his fly up.

The phone rang and he knew it was her because they were supposed to have met in the lobby ten minutes ago. He pushed off the edge of the bed and made it to the console table before the third ring.

"Mr. Culver?"

"This must be Ms. McGuire."

"Are we still on for this morning?" Her tone was all business.

"Yes, ma'am. I do apologize, but I'm running a little slow.

How about you come up and have a cup of coffee while you wait? Room service brought up a fresh pot less than half an hour ago."

"I don't mind waiting here in the lobby."

"I have a suite with a nice big parlor."

"I don't drink coffee before I run."

"Some water then?"

She hesitated. "Frankly, I make it a policy not to go up to the guest rooms."

"I see." Chase smiled wryly. That was lie number one. "I'll be down in about five minutes."

"No problem."

He heard a click, and then slowly replaced the receiver on the cradle. He expected more enthusiasm out of her. Maybe he'd pegged her wrong. Nah, he didn't think so. She'd admitted she'd come to New York looking for a singing career. Looks like he had to bait the hook again.

He found his running shoes under the teak secretary where he'd kicked them off yesterday. Bending over to pull on the shoe hurt his ribs again and he cut loose a word his mama had literally washed his mouth out with soap for when he was twelve. He still remembered the day as if it were yesterday. Not just because of the nasty taste of the soap, but because of that first look of disappointment in his God-fearing mama's eyes.

How many times before that had she begged him not to turn out like his daddy, and in that one second, to her mind, he'd taken that fork in the road. To some degree she'd been right. Chase had disappointed himself too many times to think about. He'd done things he regretted, made promises he hadn't kept. The true irony was that two months ago, when all hell had broken loose, sending his career as a cop up in smoke, none of it had been his fault. But that hadn't seemed to matter.

He pushed the thought from his mind, tucked it away in that dark corner that had already been too contaminated with hate and anger to make a difference. Today he had a job to do and it required all his concentration. The last thing he needed to do was screw up again.

Besides, this was going to be an interesting run. He hoped Dana didn't have another appointment after his because he had every intention of hijacking her.

"LET'S TAKE another route," Chase said once they entered the park. "A change of scenery."

"Sure." Dana waited until a family of four got off the path to follow a string of ducks toward the lake before she started to run. She couldn't get Kelly out of her head. This morning's timing had been awful. Dana had dozens of questions.

"You're quiet, darlin'."

"What?" She looked over at him. He hadn't shaved yet. Dark stubble covered his chin and jaw, and she thought about what Kelly and Amy had said about him not looking like a producer. Silly, of course. There was no specific look.

"Is something wrong?" With his dark eyebrows drawn together, his gaze narrowed, his eyes looked more gray than blue.

"No. Nothing." She had to stop thinking about Kelly. It wasn't just about how much she'd miss her, which was a whole other issue, but about how much the defeat on her face had shaken Dana. Kelly giving up was kind of like signaling the end of an era. Which was really crazy because Dana had long ago removed herself from the fray. So why should it affect her?

She noticed he was lagging a bit and slowed down. One of the problems with guiding men was that they often wouldn't speak up if she went too fast for them. "Five miles again?"

"That works."

"Remember, you set the pace."

He grinned. "If I keel over you should probably stop."

"I promise to dial 911 promptly."

"That would be mighty kind of you."

"It's the least I could do. After all, I do want to get paid."

Chase laughed. "You have lived in this city too long. Ah." Grimacing, he put a hand to his side.

"You okay?"

"Yeah, it's just my ribs. Old injury."

Right. She tried not to smile. "Want to slow down?"

"Just for a while."

She immediately brought them down to a brisk walk. "What happened to your ribs?"

"I tell you that and I'll have to admit to my sordid past." He gave her one of his disarming smiles. "You're the one who seems a bit off your feed today."

She hadn't heard that phrase in a while. Her dad must have used it a hundred times while she was growing up. Probably still did. "I just found out that one of my friends is thinking about leaving the city and getting a job back home."

"Home being?"

"Wisconsin."

He let out a low whistle. "Long ways off. How did she end up here?"

"Like the rest—" She stopped herself. Did she really want to open up that discussion? Actually she'd already admitted to him that she'd come to New York in search of a singing career. Bringing it up again could be a great lead-in to finding out about his meeting yesterday. "It seems like most of the friends I've made here I met standing in line for auditions."

"I see. Is she working on Broadway?"

"No. That's part of the problem."

"So she works at the hotel?"

"She hasn't decided for sure about leaving and obviously hasn't given her notice yet, so I don't feel comfortable talking about it." Trying to sound casual, she asked, "How did your meeting with the mysterious playwright go?"

He made a sound of disgust. "It got postponed until tomorrow."

"Sorry to hear that."

"That means I'll need your services for an extra day."

"I'll check my appointment book, but that shouldn't be a problem." No, the real problem was the excitement that blossomed in her chest. She didn't understand it. Certainly hadn't expected the reaction. She'd had plenty of good-looking clients over the past couple of years. Even made the mistake of dating one of them. Which absolutely wouldn't happen again.

"You ever think about going home?"

"Not really."

"What is it about New York that you love?"

Nothing readily came to mind. She had to think about it. "The energy. The cultural diversity. The food."

"Now, what do you miss about Indiana?"

"My family," she said automatically. "Clean air. Clear blue skies. Corny county fairs. And never having to worry about whether I locked my apartment door or not." She sighed. "I miss having a car, too. What about you?"

He looked surprised. "Me? I kind of flit around, so the question isn't as applicable."

"You said you've been living between Los Angeles and Houston."

"Right," he said slowly. "Guess home was never what you'd call a Norman Rockwell painting. Mama's a good woman. Not the cookie-baking type, but she ran a strict household. I still managed to give her a run for her money."

She liked the fondness in his voice when he talked about her. "Your father?"

"You mean the sperm donor?"

"Oh."

"Yeah." He thrust a hand through his hair. "That's about the only thing I fault my mama for. She never should've stayed with the worthless son of a bitch."

"I'm sorry," Dana said quietly because she didn't know what else to say. Still, she regretted saying that. It sounded too much like pity.

Chase muttered a curse, his rudeness taking her aback, but before she could say anything he sprinted ahead.

She stopped and stared, dumbfounded, and then watched him scoop up a boy, both of them tumbling onto the grass. A second later, an out-of-control skateboarder plowed past the spot where the boy had been playing with a toy truck.

"Oh, my! Toby!" A woman carrying a baby ran toward them. "Toby." She dropped to her knees, balancing the baby on one hip while checking the boy's unnaturally bent arm. "Are you okay, baby?"

"I'm fine, Mom." Toby made a disgusted face at his mother's gentle probing. Only about four, already his male ego seemed to be intact. He straightened out his arm and shook out his hand.

The young mother breathed a sigh of relief and sent Chase a grateful look. "What do you say to the nice man, Toby?"

He broke into a big grin. "That was awesome."

Chase grunted. "Right."

"Really, thank you." The mother struggled to her feet, glancing over her shoulder in the direction of the skateboarding teenager who'd barely managed to avoid a tree. "That kid is going to hurt somebody."

Chase made an attempt to get up, but sat back down again. His hand went to his ribs, and the strain in his face said it all. Dana walked over and offered him her hand. He took it, and she helped pull him to his feet.

"Thanks," he murmured.

"You really are hurt."

"It's nothing."

"Thanks, mister." Dusting the seat of his jeans, Toby tilted his head back and grinned at Chase.

"You're welcome. I hope your truck is okay."

The boy's eyes widened. "My truck." He scampered off in search of his toy, his mother close behind him.

Dana really wanted to ask more about Chase's injury. He probably shouldn't be running. "Wow, faster than a speeding bullet."

His laugh was wry. "Not exactly."

"I didn't even see that skateboarder. He came out of nowhere. You have great reflexes." They were close to a gazebo and she steered him in that direction. "You must have played football in school."

"Me? A jock? I don't think so."

She chuckled. "I didn't mean to insult you."

"I rode in a few rodeos in my time, but sports…" He scoffed.

"Over here," she said when he veered toward the path. "Let's go sit for a while."

"Why?"

"Because I can tell your side is hurting."

"Nah, I'm fine."

She didn't believe him. He looked pale, but she wasn't about to argue. "Want to just walk then?"

He led her back onto the path and resumed a brisk pace. "I want you to have dinner with me tonight."

She looked sharply at him. "I can't."

"Won't or can't?"

"Both."

He smiled. "Why not?"

"I don't date clients."

"It's only dinner. I hate eating by myself."

"It's really not a good idea."

"Why?"

Dana took a deep breath. She'd have to be out of her mind to agree, especially now that his stay here was extended. She'd broken her rule once, and the lapse in judgment had ended up breaking her heart. The jerk had turned out to be married. With three kids. Although Bradford was from Chicago, his business brought him to New York often and he'd wooed her for months before she'd given in.

He'd been romantic, sending her flowers, writing her silly charming notes, saying all the right things. They'd had dinner, gone up to his room, had sex. The next morning his wife had surprised them both. It was their tenth wedding anniversary. The look of pain and horror on the betrayed woman's face had stayed with Dana for the past two years. So had the shame. It hadn't mattered that she hadn't known he was married. And that was no way near the worst of it for her since coming to New York.

"Consider it a business dinner," Chase said, when she'd let silence stretch. "Who knows? Maybe I'll be able to talk you into getting back into singing professionally."

"Not me," she said quickly. "I have enough on my plate."

"You never know what kind of opportunities could arise."

Damn him. He'd piqued her curiosity. Not for herself, but

for Kelly. Maybe if Dana made nice she could introduce her friend to Chase. "Where did you want to eat?"

"Name it."

"Not at the hotel."

"Fine. You tell me."

She swallowed, her thoughts moving so fast she could barely think straight. She could tell herself all she wanted that she was doing this for her friend, but that was a lie. After thinking she was immune to temptation when it came to show business, he'd snagged her like a hog-tied calf at the county fair.

"FOR GOD'S SAKE, Roscoe, I've only been here for two days. No, I haven't found the ring yet." Chase held the phone away from his ear for a second and checked his reflection in the mirror. His hair was too long and his shirt collar wasn't pressed right. It kind of curled up at the tip and touched his blazer. Too late to do anything about it. He had to meet Dana for dinner in half an hour.

"You talk to the police?" Easy to picture Roscoe's ruddy face, shock of white hair and more eyebrows than three people put together. He'd made a lot of money pumping oil out of his forty-thousand acre spread, and he never let anyone forget it.

"Not yet."

"What am I paying you for, boy?"

"Expertise." If he didn't have a hefty car payment he wouldn't have considered taking on the private detective work. Chase checked his fly. All was well in that department. "Don't go telling me how to investigate this case, Roscoe. You don't want to get me riled."

"See here, that's the problem. It's just a case to you. You don't find that ring, it's gonna be my neck on Mary Lou's choppin' block."

He knew Roscoe's wife, and the man wasn't exaggerating. Of course that sweet young thing probably couldn't even boil water or find the kitchen, but Chase got the man's drift. "I don't want to talk to the locals until I get my own feel for what's going on. Tomorrow I'll meet with security." Chase went to the window, pushed aside the drapes and eyed the mounting traffic. Good thing Dana had chosen a restaurant that was only a five-minute walk from the hotel. "You know it might help if you tell me why you brought that ring here with you in the first place."

Roscoe muttered something profane. "I already told you it ain't relevant."

Chase wasn't so sure, but no use arguing. The only thing Roscoe had told him was that he'd come to New York for two days to meet with his stockbroker and find something nice for Mary Lou's birthday. It made no sense that he had the heirloom ring with him, but he wouldn't explain. Just acted real odd every time Chase questioned him about his trip.

"One more thing, Roscoe. You having an affair?"

"Go to hell." Roscoe slammed the phone down hard.

Chase flipped his cell phone shut and rubbed his assaulted ear. This case was beginning to stink worse than a pigsty. Roscoe didn't want anyone else to know about the theft, not Mary Lou, not even his insurance company. Yes, the police here in Manhattan had been given a statement, and Roscoe had painstakingly compiled a pretty good list of potential suspects for Chase to look into.

Roscoe wasn't exactly the detailed type, yet he'd included the names of every room-service waiter who had been on duty, every maid, every bellman. Because she'd had a client staying at the St. Martine the day Roscoe had arrived, even Dana's name had made the list. The guy had done some heavy-duty homework. Made Chase suspicious. If that son of a gun knew who took the ring and wasn't fessing up, he'd have more to worry about than a chopping block.

Although Chase shouldn't complain. He was getting paid well, by the day, plus expenses, so if it meant that the less Roscoe told him the longer it took to find the ring, that wasn't such a bad thing. Except, there were two problems with that. One, Chase had known Roscoe for twenty years and the guy normally couldn't keep his mouth shut about anything. Now all of a sudden you needed a crowbar to get him to open up.

Second, as nice as it was shacking up in a fancy hotel and having play dates with a beautiful woman, Chase had to get back to Dallas by the end of the week to meet with IAD again. His gaze automatically went to the screen on his cell phone. Buddy hadn't called back yet. They'd traded three calls since yesterday afternoon. It was probably nothing or his ex-partner would've been more persistent.

His thoughts returned to Roscoe. If nothing turned up tomorrow after he talked to security and the police, Chase would have to lean harder on the old man. The thing Chase hated most was surprises.

He took a final look in the mirror and tried to flatten the bent collar. But damn if Dana McGuire wasn't turning out to be quite a pleasant one.

If she was innocent, man, he was gonna feel like crap for lying to her.

4

"ARE YOU wearing perfume?" Holding a spoon and an open pint of mint chocolate chip ice cream, Lynn, Dana's roommate, poked her dark head into the bathroom and sniffed the air. "You have a date?"

Dana glared at her. "I just bought that."

"Yeah? Thanks."

Dana growled with disgust. She knew better. She absolutely knew better. What a dope. "You'd better leave me some."

"Sure." Lynn dipped the spoon into the carton. "Who's the guy?"

"Can you please use a bowl?"

"Then I'd have to wash it."

Dana shook her head. Yeah, right. The woman didn't even know where they kept the dish detergent. Man, twenty-seven was too old to have to suffer a roommate. Yet, if you lived in Manhattan there wasn't a choice. Not for her on the amount of money she made, which on the whole wouldn't have been too bad if she hadn't been saving like crazy for her new business venture. Until last month there were three of them sharing the two-bedroom flat and they were going to have to find someone to replace Lisa pretty soon in order to afford the ridiculous rent.

Maybe Kelly had the right idea. Returning to the midwest

had major pluses. Rent was relatively cheap, even if Dana chose to go to one of the larger cities. She'd have a car again, a dog and cat, maybe even a date once in a while. But the downside was huge—the humiliation of admitting that she simply hadn't been able to cut it in the real world.

The true irony was that she hadn't been the one so hot to leave the small farming community where she'd known every last kid in the small grade school, and at fourteen, shared her very first kiss with Bobby Miller, the captain of the football team. Her mother, her teachers, her high-school guidance counselor, even Maude Maubry, the town's librarian, had urged Dana to set her sights on bigger things.

She checked to make sure she hadn't gotten any lip gloss on her teeth, ran a brush through her hair one last time and then exited the tiny ancient bathroom that desperately needed some repairs to the rusty pipes and loose tiles.

Lynn backed down the short hallway. "Since you won't be home tonight, can I borrow your—?"

"No."

"You didn't let me finish."

Dana edged past her, noting wryly that the ice cream was almost gone. "Have you ever returned anything you've borrowed from me?"

Lynn frowned. "I think so."

"Think again." Dana grabbed the small black purse she'd hung off her bedroom doorknob. Weird even to carry a purse. Normally she stuck keys, money and her cell phone in her jeans pocket, or in a fanny pack if she wore only Spandex running shorts.

"You coming home tonight?"

"Yes." She noticed the disappointment in Lynn's black-outlined eyes. "So do not touch my stuff."

Dana left the apartment without another word, recalling a time when she would never have spoken to another human being like that. Good old Dana would have given anyone the shirt off her back. All they needed to do was ask. In fact, they didn't have to say a word. She'd volunteer. Even if it were minus ten degrees outside and she had nothing else to wear.

She'd been the consummate good girl. Church-going. God-fearing. Perfect manners. Valedictorian of her class. Blessed with both looks and modest talent. The role model for every girl in town. Much to her chagrin, she'd been the one all the other parents compared their kids to. Her biggest fault had been her deep-seated foolish desire to please everyone. Her biggest secret was that she was basically shy.

With the possible exception of her father, no one had seemed to see that side of her. She'd just smiled a lot and allowed everyone their assumptions. Being on stage had been remarkably easy because she felt as if she was someone else entirely, and that's where she'd fooled everyone. She'd almost fooled herself. She'd started to believe the hype that she was special and needed to spread her wings.

The truth was, she hadn't changed much. Below the cool surface she was still that shy girl from Smallville, Indiana, population fifteen hundred and thirty-six, only after Marilyn Wilson had had triplets last year. If Dana were brave enough to dig deep, she'd probably find that she didn't belong in a place like New York. But the longer she stayed the harder it was to go home. Instead, she mailed her letter every other week, phoning her parents on alternate weeks, keeping the calls short, never disabusing them of the idea that long distance still cost an arm and a leg.

At the corner she hailed a cab, not wanting to pit out by walking in the sticky humid weather. She hated that she'd put herself in this funk. It was stupid. By now everyone back home knew she hadn't made it big, after all. Just because she hadn't uttered the words didn't mean reality hadn't roosted. She wasn't responsible for their disappointment. She had her own to deal with.

No, no, she'd put all that angst to rest. She wouldn't even be thinking about any of it if it weren't for Chase Culver. He'd stirred up the pot. Still, she knew better than to resurrect hope.

A cab stopped for her and she slid inside, giving the cabbie the restaurant's address. She squared her shoulders. This was going to be a good test of her resolve. See if she'd really made the peace she thought she had. And yet who knew, maybe he just might have something worthwhile to offer.

CHASE ARRIVED a few minutes early and convinced the hostess to give him a nice quiet table in the corner of the restaurant, from where he had a clear view of the entrance. The place was simple, wooden chairs and tables set with laminated place-mats listing New York trivia questions instead of tablecloths. On the walls were pictures of different parts of Manhattan, circa mid-nineteen hundreds. The only nod to formality was the crisp red linen napkins.

When the waitress came by he ordered a beer while he waited for Dana. He had no idea where she lived and with the crazy traffic out there, there was no telling when she'd make it. But the waitress had no sooner left the table than he saw Dana walk in. His breathing literally faltered.

With her hair down, bouncing around her shoulders, it looked much blonder than when it was pulled back in a pony-tail. And the dress…breathtaking. Simple, black and sleeve-less, hugging her every curve, it nearly made his heart stop altogether. The hem ended about five inches above her knees, and he didn't know how it was possible, but her legs looked even better than when she wore running shorts.

Every man in the joint, from eighteen to eighty, turned to watch her walk past their tables. Not that he wasn't a gentleman, though he wasn't the type to get up and pull out a woman's chair in a circumstance like this, but he was on his feet before he knew it and had her chair out and waiting before she got to him.

"Thank you," she said, her cheeks turning pink. "You didn't have to do that."

He felt as if he was in eleventh grade again. Every guy in school dreamed about taking Rebecca Weaver to the homecoming dance. Including him. Naturally she went with the captain of the football team. But she'd saved a dance for Chase, whispered something sweet in his ear and kissed him on the lips. He thought he'd won the lottery. Holding on to that night had gotten him through many a dry spell, when all he had to warm him was rosy palm and her five sisters, but that night at the dance didn't hold a candle to this very moment.

The creamy vanilla fragrance drifting up from her hair held him rooted for a second too long and as soon as he realized he was hovering, he released her chair and reclaimed his own.

Their eyes met, and she smiled shyly.

"You look stunning," he said.

"Thank you," she murmured, the pink returning to her cheeks. She actually seemed uncomfortable with the compliment. It wasn't an act. She couldn't be that good. Could she? "You clean up pretty well yourself."

He smiled. "No comparison."

She made a face. "Stop it."

"Okay." He put up his hands, and noticed the waitress returning with his beer. "Sorry I didn't wait, but I ordered a drink. I wasn't sure when you'd get here. What would you like?"

The waitress arrived, set down his glass and while she poured the beer, smiled at Dana. "What can I get you?"

"I'll have the same," she said, surprising him.

"I thought you were more the wine type," he said when the waitress had left.

"Funny, I was thinking the same about you."

"Me? A good ole boy from Texas. Bite your tongue." He pushed the bottle and glass toward her, belatedly remembering that as a big-shot producer he probably should've ordered wine. "Be my guest. I can wait."

"Tell you what…" She topped off the foaming glass and then handed it to him. "We'll split it." And then she tipped the bottle to her lips.

Chase grinned. This was his kind of woman. "I would've taken the bottle."

She smiled back. "Beat you to it."

Moisture clung to her pale pink lips, making them glisten. Or maybe she'd done something to them. Used some tinted gloss maybe, but nothing much. Altering perfection would be a crime. He'd have to arrest her. Take her back to his room in handcuffs. Secure her to the bedposts to make sure she didn't get away.

His slacks suddenly got uncomfortably snug and he shifted positions. Damn, he had to stay on track. Too easy to forget why he'd asked her to dinner. He took a cool sip and leaned back. "Tell me about this friend of yours. The one who wants to pack it in and go home."

She looked startled, and then shrugged a slim shoulder. "Kelly's amazingly talented. She dances, sings, acts."

He knew that name. She was a hotel employee. The assistant concierge, maybe? He kept an impassive face, mentally filing away the name. "Has she worked on Broadway?"

"She's had a few roles. Mostly small ones, but one of the plays she did lasted for nearly a year. It's just not easy getting cast. I don't have to tell you that it's a cutthroat business."

"Yep, a lot of money at stake."

She tilted her head to the side and studied him in a way that made him nervous. Like she was going to ask him a question he didn't know how to answer. "What made you decide to get involved in show business?"

"Good question." He frowned thoughtfully, pretending to give the matter serious consideration. "I'm afraid I don't have a very noble answer."

"Fame and money is a given."

"This industry is fickle. Profit isn't a guarantee. It could cost you big-time."

"True."

The waitress returned with Dana's beer and asked to take their orders. But neither of them had looked at the menu yet. As soon as the woman left to check on another table, Chase picked up his menu hoping Dana would forget the nature of their conversation.

"Come on. Now I'm curious."

He stupidly hadn't anticipated the question, but he'd learned doing undercover work that sticking as close to the truth as possible reduced your risk of exposure. "I was bored."

"Ah. The curse of the idle rich."

"Now, now, darlin'. You know boredom isn't only a rich man's affliction."

"Okay, you're right." Her lips curved in a cheeky smile. "They just get to be bored without worrying about paying the mortgage."

"Touché."

"At least you're honest," she said, picking up her menu.

He flinched and quickly directed his attention to the list of entrées. Maybe dinner hadn't been such a good idea. No, this was a good opportunity. As long as he retained control of the conversation.

Nothing on the menu was too pricey, particularly by Manhattan standards. He liked that she'd chosen this place even though she thought he had deep pockets. "Any recommendations?"

"Everything is good." She closed her menu and set it aside.

"What are you having?"

"Blackened chicken salad."

Should've known she was one of those salad kind of gals, low-fat dressing on the side, no doubt. Why it disappointed him he couldn't say. Him, he was a having a great big porterhouse steak.

As soon as he closed his menu the waitress appeared again and took their order. He asked for another beer, but Dana declined. A smarter man would've followed her lead. He had to meet her at ten tomorrow and run another five miles. Although, if he got enough information tonight, there really would be no reason to see her.

Their eyes met, hers so beautiful his groin stirred. Who was he kidding? No way he'd pass up a chance to see her again. He smiled and went for his beer.

"How's your side?"

"Better."

"How did you say you hurt it?"

"A man can humble himself only so much in one night."

She smiled. "Must be a pretty juicy story."

He wouldn't call it that. But he couldn't very well admit he'd been part of an undercover sting that had gone bad. One that might have shot his career to hell and back.

Focus. He couldn't start replaying that old tape. Might as

well call it a night if his mind had started going to that bad neighborhood. "Let's get back to your friend. She has a résumé and portfolio, I presume."

At his abruptness, Dana blinked. "Sure."

"Okay." He paused, trying to gather his thoughts. "After my meeting tomorrow I'll know more about how close I am to sealing this deal."

"Great." Dana seemed nervous suddenly, her hand trembling slightly as she picked up her bottle of beer. "If it works out for you and you'd like to talk to my friend, I could arrange for the two of you to meet."

"You sound more like her agent."

She smiled. "She's had a tough go of it lately, and I hate to see her give up."

A loud group of six sat at the table next to them, the three guys arguing over yesterday's Mets' game and sounding as if they'd already been partying half the afternoon.

Chase leaned across the table toward Dana. Her lips were really something, full and pouty, but natural-looking. "What about you?"

"What about me?" she asked warily.

"Aren't you interested?"

She hesitated. "That phase of my life is over. I've moved on."

"That's a shame," he said, relieved because he didn't have to feel like a jerk for getting her hopes up.

She briefly looked away. "What about you? What will you do if this deal fails?"

"Failure is never an option." Yeah, easy to sound confident when you were full of crap. When you didn't know if you were even going to have a job next month. What the hell. He was kind of liking this private-dick stuff, especially the expense-account part.

"Good attitude. I hope it works for you." She smiled, but it didn't erase the trace of bitterness in her voice.

Brought him back to the reason he was here. Bitterness could change a person. Make them do things they weren't proud of, or worse, make them think it was their God-given right to take what they wanted. Like turn to thieving to support a lifestyle they felt they'd been cheated out of. He studied Dana as she stared into her beer, her blond hair falling forward like a sheet of expensive fine silk.

Did she fit that profile? Did she feel she deserved more than life had dished out? Did it matter that a woman like her could get a man to give her anything she wanted? She wouldn't even have to work at it. Just bat those beautiful eyes. Or maybe she liked more of a challenge. Wanted a more active role. Could be she was working with someone.

Hell, that was an angle he hadn't considered yet. She seemed chummy with some of the hotel staff. Maybe her job was to distract the target while an accomplice snatched the goods. Made sense. The possibility was certainly worth considering.

The idea grated on him more than it should. He didn't want her to be involved. His lack of objectivity really got to him. Hadn't he learned his lesson in the past year? Of course it wasn't as if she were a serious suspect yet. But until she could be eliminated, she stayed on the list. When the eliminations were done, the last man standing ended up in cuffs.

After poking around yesterday, he had his eye on a room-service waiter and a maid. Both had opportunity and knowledge of the ring. He knew the maid had been on the same floor at the time of the other theft. The waiter's timeline hadn't been confirmed.

Still, the fact that Dana had lied about not going up to the guest floors nagged at him. He knew that wasn't true because

Roscoe had seen her. Which brought him back to his original suspicion that she did know Roscoe. The idea that they could've been intimate made him queasy.

"You've gotten awfully quiet," she said, toying with her napkin so that it was beginning to shred. "Anything wrong?"

"I was thinking about your friend. When did she decide to leave New York?"

Dana frowned. "Why?"

"Because if I go forward, I need people who are committed to the film. If she already has a job lined up back home—"

Dana laughed. "Trust me. If you have a role for her, she'll commit."

That didn't go as planned. "This decision…was it a sudden one?"

"I think so." She took a pensive sip. "But I don't really know. I haven't talked to her much since she dropped the bomb. Actually, I was going to see if she'd meet me this evening and fill me in. That was before you asked me to dinner."

He smiled. "I'm glad you didn't turn me down."

"Me, too," she said quietly, briefly meeting his eyes before looking at the napkin she'd been working on.

He forced his attention on the business at hand. "So this friend of yours, she isn't leaving because of an old boyfriend or job or anything in particular?"

Dana gave him an odd look. She settled back, her posture on the defensive side. "She received a letter from her mother telling her about a job that's opened up, a pretty good job, apparently."

"Ah. Not show business," he said, absently. That didn't mean she didn't have another motive for wanting a quick exit.

"Oh, no. She has a business degree."

"What about you? Did you go to college?"

Dana nodded. "Yep. Just a junior college near my home for two years and then I finished up at the university. I have a teaching degree so I can always rely on that."

"You don't look like any teacher I ever had."

She rolled her eyes. "What about you? Before you got bored," she said, the corners of her mouth twitching. "What did you do?"

"I dropped out of school."

Her eyebrows went up.

"Not high school. College. In the middle of my third year."

"Holy moly, that must've made your parents real happy."

"My mom was ready to run me up a flagpole." He went with the truth. Besides, being easier to keep track of, for some reason, he didn't want to lie to her anymore than he could help it. "My dad didn't care one way or the other."

Her expression softened. "Was he present in your life?"

"When it suited him. Hey, no puppy-dog eyes for me. The less I saw of the old man the better I liked it." He meant it, although he regretted offering that much information.

Fortunately, the waitress arrived with their food, and he immediately dug into his steak. Dana didn't press him to talk more, which was a good thing because he had no intention of getting that personal again. Better he keep his focus on the job and not her incredible blue eyes.

5

DANA ORDERED cheesecake for dessert, ignoring Chase's grin when she asked for extra chocolate drizzle. That was the up side of exercising a couple of times a day…she got to over-indulge sometimes. Besides, she doubted there'd be any ice cream left once she got home.

After Chase paid the check, refusing her offer to cover the tip, they left the restaurant. Just outside, people waiting for tables had formed a line, causing a bottleneck. The pressure of Chase's hand at the small of her back as he guided them to an opening on the sidewalk created a pleasant tingling that started at the base of her spine and radiated to her breasts and the inside of her thighs. It was crazy because it was a casual touch. Nothing sexual about it at all.

"Do you need to get home right away?" he asked, his mouth close to her ear.

"I have an early appointment." She sidestepped a teenage couple who were so busy kissing as they walked that they nearly plowed into them. The move broke her contact with Chase.

"I thought maybe we could take a walk through the park." He came up alongside her, their shoulders touching as they walked.

"That won't count as your run for tomorrow."

"Yeah, but you probably should work off some of that cheesecake."

"Hey."

He grinned. "It's safe, isn't it? The park after dark?"

"For whom? After that crack I could ditch you in Mugger's Alley."

They stopped at the intersection to wait for a crossing light. "Is that a real place?"

"I just made it up." The backs of their hands touched and she moved hers away. "I think I'd better call it a night."

He looked down at her, his mouth lifting in a slow, seductive smile. "Sure is a shame to waste all that beautiful moonlight."

"It won't be wasted," she said sweetly. "I'll enjoy every bit of it on my walk home."

"Who knew that beneath that angelic face lay a cruel woman."

Dana grinned at the deflated look on his face. "However, the hotel is on my way."

He sobered. "You're not seriously thinking of walking."

"I do it all the time."

"It's not safe."

"Yes, it is, or I wouldn't do it. It's not like I live in the slums."

"That's not the point."

"I'm sorry. Did I mislead you? Did you think my mode of transportation was up for discussion?" She didn't know whether to be amused or annoyed.

Chase made a wounded sound. "I'll shut up."

She hid a smile. He was just too damn cute with his crooked grin and his hooded blue eyes. Up close like this she could see that they were really more gray, it was just that his hair was so dark it made his eyes look lighter. Even though he wasn't classically handsome, something about his square jaw, dimpled chin and the way his mouth seemed to droop a little on the left appealed to her in a big way.

The light changed and she was about to cross when Chase grabbed her hand. "Come on, darlin'. I was a hero today. I deserve a short walk."

Dana laughed. "I thought modesty was also hero criteria."

"Not when you're from Texas," he said, winking, and when he led her in the direction of the park, she didn't object.

But she did free her hand. She didn't want him getting the wrong idea. "Let's stick close to Fifth Avenue."

"Is that on the way to your place?"

She darted him a look, suspicious of his motive for asking. If he thought for one minute she'd ask him up to her apartment... She quickly realized his question was innocent. "No, that area's too high-rent for me."

"Yeah, I guess it would cost more to live near the park," he said absently, and then lifted his gaze to the clear sky. "It sure is a beautiful night. Too bad we can't see more stars. Back home the sky would be lit like a birthday cake full of candles."

"I would've thought Houston has too much light pollution to see that many stars."

"I wasn't talking about Houston. I grew up about a hundred and twenty miles outside of Dallas in a small town just like you."

"Really?" That was interesting. She would never have guessed. They left the street and headed into the park, taking the same path as this morning. "You must've left a long time ago."

"Why?" He looked at her with precisely that expression that made her wonder about him, a sprinkling of charm, a dash of cynicism that gave him a rough edge.

"I don't know why I said that." She lied, but she preferred to think of it as good manners.

His slow, knowing smile had her wishing she'd turned down the walk. "It's the business, darlin', it changes a person. Can make you callous if you're not careful."

She stared into the darkness, embarrassed that he'd read her thoughts.

"Hasn't seemed to affect you any," he said quietly. "Why is that?"

She laughed humorlessly to herself. Oh, she'd changed, all right. "What makes you think it hasn't?"

He shrugged. "Because you're a nice lady. You're concerned about your friend. I know that's the only reason you had dinner with me."

Heat surged up her neck and into her face. Good thing it was dark. "That isn't true."

"Then why did you agree to meet me?"

She shook her head. Damned if she did, damned if she didn't. "Very tricky."

He laughed. "That wasn't the plan. But now I'm curious."

They passed a couple sitting on a bench who really should've gotten the proverbial room. Dana kept her face straight ahead, but couldn't ignore the yearning their intimacy stirred in her belly. It had been a long time since she'd gone on a date or met a man who she wanted to kiss like that. Too long.

She bet Chase was a heck of a good kisser.

The sudden thought startled her. Warning bells went off in her head. Talk about heading in the wrong direction. She definitely could not go there. He was not only a client, but a possible business connection. Which should matter not a whit to her, darn it. She was done with all that. Hadn't she told herself a million times that show business wasn't for her? Too much heartache and disappointment. She was on a much safer track, one that actually could provide her with a future.

"Um, could we save the running for tomorrow morning?" The amusement in Chase's voice made her grit her teeth.

She immediately slowed down her marathon pace, murmuring, "Sorry."

"Dana?" He touched her arm.

She didn't want to look at him.

"Why did you agree to have dinner with me?" His touch turned to a caress, and reluctantly she stopped and met his gaze.

"I really, really don't usually do this…see clients socially." This was crazy. They were standing in the middle of the path.

One side of his mouth lifted. "Is that assertion supposed to make me less curious?"

Her resolve was weakening. The longer she looked up into his darkening eyes, his lids slowly lowering, the more she wanted that kiss. "One other time, I broke the rule, and it turned out disastrously."

He hooked a finger under her chin. "Nothing to do with us."

"There is no us," she whispered.

He lifted her chin.

"Wait." She swallowed hard.

"Yes?"

"Are you married?"

He reared his head back slightly. "No."

"You swear?"

"I swear."

She studied his face, although she didn't know what she hoped to see. If he was lying he was good at it.

"I was engaged once," he volunteered.

"What happened?"

His mouth twisted wryly. "The lady wised up."

Dana blinked, not expecting that much honesty. Did she

even want to know the reason the engagement went bad? It was only one kiss, after all.

Lowering his head the final few inches, he brushed her lips with his. She put a hand on his hard chest. He accepted the invitation by touching his tongue to the corner of her mouth and then running it across the seam of her lips. Reflexively, she opened to him.

Despite his boldness, he took his time, touching his tongue to hers, to the inside of her cheek, the roof of her mouth, and gliding across her front teeth. As if helpless to respond, she stood there, a passive participant, as he learned her mouth.

He was the one who stopped, pulling his head back to look at her, and running his thumb across her lower lip. If she could move, she probably would've run out of the park, all the way to her apartment. Throw the deadbolt on her front door. Hide until she knew he was on a plane far away from New York City.

Or at least until she regained her sanity.

HE WAS out of his mind. What the hell was he thinking? He stared down at her upturned face, full of both doubt and desire, and which surely reflected his own. He couldn't resist touching her glistening bottom lip one more time before lowering his hand.

"Probably not one of my better ideas," he said, his voice still thick.

"Me, too," she whispered, moving away from him.

"I should probably regret it."

She smiled faintly. "We should get back."

"Yeah."

Voices came from behind them. He glanced over his shoulder and saw a whole group of young people on the path headed in their direction.

"We don't have to go back the same way," Dana said, already moving toward the fork on the right. "We can get back on Sixty-third Street this way."

He fell into step beside her, neither of them talking for a long stretch. Finally he asked, "Are we good?"

She nodded.

He wasn't convinced, but he said nothing. They both needed some distance, probably a good night's sleep, although he wasn't sure how successful he'd be at that right now. Didn't matter that intellectually he knew kissing her had been bad for his concentration. His body had other ideas. Good thing she seemed more coolheaded about the whole thing, or he might not have stopped. He might've talked her into going back to his room. Getting naked. Letting him taste every silky sweet inch of her.

Damn.

He pulled the shirt collar away from his clammy neck. There he went. Getting all worked up again.

"Dana?"

Tentatively, she looked over at him, the light shining on her face illuminating her flushed cheeks.

"What happened with that other client?"

She briefly closed her eyes and then looked away.

He'd known before he opened his mouth that that was a boneheaded thing to ask, but he couldn't seem to help himself. "I've already figured out the bum must have been married." Chase was a lot of unflattering things, but he never messed with married women.

"I didn't know he was married."

"I pretty much guessed that, too. I know it's none of my business—"

"No, it's not." She gave him a small smile that softened her abruptness. "I don't want to talk about it."

He nodded, feeling like a chump for bringing it up. Fortunately they reached the street, so the awkward moment passed quickly. The quiet neighborhood was more residential, but in the distance he could see the intersection where they'd entered the park. It wouldn't be long before she'd go her way, and he'd go his. He hoped tomorrow they could get back on solid ground again.

He cleared his throat. "So, are you a baseball fan?"

She looked at him in surprise, her lush pink mouth parting slightly, and then she laughed. "I promise. We're okay."

"Right." He stuffed his hands into his pockets. Now probably wasn't the time to tell her he really wanted to kiss her again. God, she had perfect lips.

"Look, it's late so I think I'll grab a cab, after all." Just as one pulled out of a side street, she stuck her hand out and flagged down the driver. "I can drop you at the hotel."

Startled, he shook his head. "I'm going to walk."

The cab pulled up at the curb. She beat him to the handle and opened the door. "Are you sure? The St. Martine is on my way."

Relieved that it appeared she wasn't trying to ditch him, he pulled a wad of bills out of his pocket. "No, I need the fresh air."

"Here? Good luck." She smiled, but then sobered when she saw that he intended to pass the driver a twenty. She put a hand on his. "No, thank you."

He wanted to argue just so she wouldn't move her hand. Was every part of her as soft as her satiny cheeks? "I'd like to—"

"No. I've got it. Tomorrow at ten?"

He nodded and stepped back.

She said nothing else, just got inside the back of the cab, and he closed the door.

The car sped off and he walked in the same direction,

watching until the taillights disappeared into a sea of cabs and a blur of red brake lights.

Just as well she'd left. He still had work to do tonight. If he didn't quit screwing around, in good conscience, he'd have to personally eat some of his expense-account money. Couldn't let Roscoe keep paying thirteen-hundred a night for the junior suite just because Chase had dragged out the investigation. Not to mention the stiff price for a beer at the hotel bar.

Although the brew he'd nursed last night had been worth every penny. He hoped the same big mouth was tending bar. God bless unions. The guy had to be pushing seventy, had worked at the St. Martine for forty-four years and knew every detail of every rumor down to the general manager's brand of skivvies.

Thanks to old Herbert, Chase knew which employees liked to bet the ponies, and which ones headed for the crap tables in Atlantic City on their days off. He'd also found out that the doormen and bellmen made small fortunes and that most of them had wisely invested in real estate over the years and could retire at the drop of a hat.

What Chase found particularly interesting was that the new assistant manager had a taste for fine things and liked to put on airs. But the truth was, he lived in Brooklyn in a flat with two roommates and pretended to take a cab to work, but had been spotted getting off the subway. He'd told conflicting stories about where he'd come from, and inserted the fact that he'd gone to prestigious Cornell University into every conversation possible. Herbert had found out from a clerk in Human Resources that the guy had gotten there on a scholarship.

Yep, the bartender had proved to be a gold mine. Chase had purposefully left him a huge tip that he'd charged to his suite long before he actually left the bar. The amount must've impressed Herbert because he kept singing like a whole chorus of canaries. Unfortunately, he had nothing to say about Dana. Or maybe it was fortunate. He'd heard of her because just about every guy in the building had the hots for her, but he only worked nights and had never actually seen her.

About a block from the hotel, Chase got out his cell phone. Buddy would be home by now, or at Homer's Bar and Grill, a place he'd frequented since Darlene and the kids had left him five months ago. Chase hit speed dial, but the call went straight to voice mail. He left another message even though he pretty much knew what Buddy wanted and if he called back right away, it would be difficult to talk about such a sensitive matter while sitting at the hotel bar.

Turned out it didn't matter. When Chase got to the lounge he found out Herbert was off tonight and tomorrow. The woman who'd replaced him behind the bar was a sweet young thing, but useless in the information department.

Without finishing his beer, Chase left and wandered around the unusually crowded lobby for a few minutes. He recognized both women working behind the front desk. They were normal nightshift personnel, but one of them had been on vacation at the time of the theft. The other woman had been off that day. The day clerk, Amy, who covered the shift two nights a week, had been on duty.

But he'd also learned that it was unusual for the front-desk people to be on the guest-room floors. Security, housekeeping, room service and engineering were the departments that had people who moved around the hotel enough to make them suspects. Two-thirds of them had already been eliminated.

He'd started toward the front desk to see what he could stir up when his cell phone rang. Seeing that it was Buddy calling, he headed instead for the elevators and the privacy of his room. "Hey," he answered.

"You having too good a time in New York that you don't answer your calls?"

Chase shook his head. The elevator doors opened and he got in and pressed the button to his floor. "Right."

"Just ragging on you." Buddy took a loud drag off his cigarette. "Darlene and me have been talking about her coming home. I don't wanna piss her off so when I'm with her I turn off the phone."

"Good move. What else is going on?"

"IAD wants to talk to me again."

Chase frowned. Internal affairs had already crawled up everybody's ass, he knew, including Buddy's. Besides, Chase thought they were close to a ruling. "About what?"

"I don't know. I got the word last night."

"When do you meet with them?"

"Tomorrow. What do you want me to tell 'em?"

"The truth."

Buddy snorted. "Man, that hasn't gotten you far, know what I mean?"

Chase arrived at his floor and got out his key card. "Yeah, but all I've got is the truth."

"You'd think that'd be enough, huh? I dunno, the captain is being too quiet on this one. Something stinks."

He opened his door, and as soon as he got inside he started shrugging out of his jacket while he held the phone. "It has from the beginning..." He noticed his running shoes right away. They weren't where he'd left them. His gaze went to the shelf above the mini bar where the safe was. "Buddy, I've got to go," he said and disconnected the call. Shit, someone had been in his room.

6

DANA ARRIVED at the hotel at exactly ten the next morning. Kelly was talking to a guest, and today was Amy's day off. No sign of Chase. She wondered if he was feeling as sluggish as she was. She'd gotten to bed early enough, but getting to sleep had been a whole other matter. At about four-thirty she'd finally dozed off. Tired of replaying the kiss, her brain had shut down in self-defense.

Even at fourteen when she'd kissed Bobby Miller for the first time she hadn't been so ridiculous about it. Okay, maybe she had, but that was thirteen years ago. Last night was one insignificant kiss. No big deal.

Right. She pulled off the sunglasses that she'd hooked onto the neckline of her oversized T-shirt, and slipped them on. Not so much to hide the evidence of a sleepless night, but to hide, period. She'd known better than to have dinner with Chase. She was far too attracted to him. The kiss had been inevitable, and now everything had changed between them. She could pretend all she wanted that it didn't matter.

When she saw him coming from the elevators, she decided to step outside and wait for him by the doors. He wasn't exactly moving fast, and she wondered what kind of night he'd had. But of course the kiss probably hadn't fazed him.

"Mornin'," he said, unsmiling.

Her heart plummeted. "Good morning." She didn't know what else to say so she led him outside. Should she apologize? After all, she was the one who should've been more professional.

The sidewalk was surprisingly deserted and with the way clear, she automatically started at a fast clip.

"Slow down there, darlin'." He smiled then, a kind of lop-sided rendition, and put a familiar hand on her arm. "I could've used one less beer last night."

"I could've done without the cheesecake," she said, his touch prompting mixed feelings. On the one hand, she was glad he wasn't out of sorts over last night, but on the other, he couldn't think that anything had changed between them.

Worst of all was her physical reaction to his casual touch. Like a sunflower drawn to the sun, her entire body longed to lean into him. She wanted him to trace her lips again, run the back of his hand down her cheek. The whole thing was insane.

"At the risk of sounding like a total wuss, I don't think I'm going to do much running today."

"Did you want to cancel?" she asked, disappointed. "I won't charge you for today."

"No." He gave an emphatic shake of his head. "I just meant we should stick to a slow jog. That's all."

"Okay. But if you want to skip it altogether—"

"No way."

At his adamant tone, she held back a smile. "Maybe we should try a change of scenery. The Hudson River is another route I—"

"No, that would take too long. I have a lot to do today."

"All right."

They got to the corner and although they had the walk signal, they had to wait while three cabs flew through the red light before they crossed. "Sorry if I seemed short. I didn't get much sleep."

Dana immediately looked the other way, her mouth going dry. She did not want to have this conversation. Ignoring what had happened was much better.

"Someone broke into my room last night."

She swung her head around to look at him. "While you were there?"

"When we were at dinner."

"Oh, no. Did they take anything?"

"No." He stared back at her, his expression oddly blank. "Did you know about the thefts at the St. Martine?"

She hesitated. She hadn't even said anything to her roommate about what was going on at the hotel. Talking about it felt somehow disloyal. A lot of the staff would be hurt if business fell off. "The employees are forbidden to discuss it, but I've heard things," she said slowly. "What's security doing about last night?"

"I talked to the guard on duty. He took a statement. When I get back I'm talking to the head guy."

"You're lucky nothing was taken from you."

"Yeah, real lucky," he said, his tone grim.

"I'm sorry. I didn't mean to sound flip. I'm sure you still felt violated."

He studied her for a long, uncomfortable moment. "I did."

"I'm sure. You know if word gets out, it's really going to affect the hotel's business." Dana glanced over her shoulder. But there wasn't a soul close enough to have overheard. "I have clients from hotels all over Manhattan, but the St. Martine has been particularly good to me and I'd hate to see them hurt by this."

"Well, they sure as hell had better do something about it."

"Security questions all the employees who were working during the time of the theft." She shrugged. "They've even wanted to talk to me."

His gaze narrowed. "Why?"

"Because I'm there five or six days a week."

"How many thefts have been reported?"

She cringed, not really wanting to give him the information. "Four or five, I think."

He let out a low whistle. "Must be an inside job."

She didn't say anything. Although it wasn't as if she hadn't thought the same thing. But she knew almost everyone there, at least by sight or hearsay, and she didn't want to believe that any of them could be involved.

"See that bench over there?" He pointed to the one facing the lake where the ducks bobbed for pieces of bread being scattered by two young children and their mother. "It's got our names on it."

"Seriously? You want to sit?"

"I want to sit."

She sighed. "Wish you would've said something earlier, I would've grabbed some coffee."

He hooked a thumb over his shoulder. "We passed a bagel shop. Wanna go back?"

They got to the bench, and she sat first. "Too late." And then she quickly put a hand to her mouth to cover a yawn.

"You're tired, too."

He lowered himself beside her, sitting much closer than he should have considering their professional relationship. His thigh brushed hers, and then he leaned and stretched his arm along the seat behind her. Anyone passing by would get entirely the wrong impression, assuming anyone cared, which around here they didn't. But that wasn't the point.

She furtively shifted a couple of inches away. "I'm not really tired," she lied. "But I did have two other appointments this morning already."

He drew his head back in surprise. "You ran?"

"Private personal training sessions."

"Ah, so your clients did all the work." His eyes reflected the blue from the lake and sky. The direct sunlight revealed faint lines that fanned out from the corners of his eyes and a tiny scar on his cheekbone that she hadn't noticed before.

"Yep, and I get to charge them for it."

His mouth curved. "Some racket."

"Legal, too. See? My life isn't so bad."

The smile faded, his dark eyebrows drawing together in a slight frown, his gaze capturing hers. If he tried to kiss her again, she didn't know what she'd do. Of course, she'd turn her head. Make sure he understood that last night had been a mistake. That there would be no repeat. No matter how tempting…

"I have a hypothetical question," he said slowly. "If you knew who was involved with the thefts, would you come forward?"

"What?" She drew away from him. "What kind of question is that?" Affronted, she got up, but he grabbed her hand.

"That came out wrong."

Her heart had raced all the way up her throat. She pulled free of him, but she stayed put. "I sincerely hope so."

"Sit, please. I'll explain."

She slowly lowered herself onto the bench, keeping a safe distance from him. Not that she was tempted any longer. She was ticked. His explanation had better be good.

"You guys all seem to be a close-knit group. I'm wondering how far the staff would go to cover for someone if they knew what was going on."

"First off, you're right, that came out very wrong. That was an awful question." She sent him a resentful look. "And frankly, rephrased, I still don't like it. I can't see why an innocent person would cover up for someone."

His look said he thought she was being naive. "There are many reasons, believe me."

She folded her arms across her chest. "Then you know more about it than I do."

"I'm talking about extortion, intimidation, blackmail, that sort of thing."

She frowned at him. "Who are you?"

He looked away, roughly pushing a hand through his unruly hair. "A little over the top, huh?"

"A little," she said drily. Obviously the break-in had upset him, and she decided to cut him some slack. "For what it's worth, you probably now have the safest room in the hotel. I bet security hasn't left your floor."

"Yeah." He seemed moderately appeased. "Can I ask another question, or have you had it with me?"

"Both. What?"

He hesitated, indecision apparent in his eyes. "Did you tell anyone you were having dinner with me last night?"

"No." She didn't like that question, either, but she understood why he asked.

"Not even the front-desk gals you hang out with?"

"To tell you the truth, I would've been too embarrassed to tell them." Dana sighed. "They know about my policy of keeping my professional life separate."

His gaze roamed her face, and then lingered on her lips. "I'm glad you made an exception last night."

"Which obviously didn't turn out well."

He grunted and rested his elbows just above his knees, his attention going toward the lake.

She really wished she hadn't said that. But it was totally reflexive, a kind of self-defense. The way he'd looked at her made her nervous. Made her not trust herself. "I'm sorry this has ruined your trip."

"What?" He straightened and looked at her again. "No. No. It's fine. Kind of made things interesting."

She laughed. "Interesting?"

He shrugged. "I've always been a mystery buff. I like unraveling the whys and whos." He flashed her that disarming smile. "I'm still pissed, but I gotta look on the bright side."

"Good for you," she said, meaning it. She elbowed him lightly in the ribs. "Want to move?"

He flinched slightly. "Sure."

"Oh, did I get you?" She briefly covered her mouth, and then started to touch his side, but quickly retreated. She'd forgotten about his injury.

"It's okay." He covered her hand with his, squeezing gently. Probably to keep her from doing any more damage. "Come on." He rose first and pulled her to her feet, keeping her hand prisoner.

She ended up face-to-face with him, mere inches separating their lips. "I can't do this," she whispered.

"Doesn't mean I don't want to kiss you senseless," he whispered back. And then he smiled again. That totally unfair smile that scrambled her brain. "How about dinner in my suite tonight?"

BY THE TIME they returned to the hotel, she still hadn't given him an answer. It should've been simple. No. Absolutely not. Dinner was bad enough, but room service in his suite? Crazy. So why hadn't she just spat it out?

If she didn't have to meet another guest at the St. Martine in thirty minutes, she would've skipped the hotel altogether. But they entered the lobby together and if she wasn't annoyed enough, the first person she saw was Kyle standing near the front desk talking to Kelly.

Before she could veer off in the opposite direction, he spotted her and headed straight for them.

"That's the assistant manager," she said quickly before Chase said something she wouldn't want Kyle to hear.

Chase's gaze tracked the shorter blond man's approach. "The pretty boy?"

"That's him," she murmured, and forced a smile. "Hello, Kyle."

"Just the person I wanted to see." Kyle's eyes made a brief detour to her breasts, nothing overt, but enough to make her skin crawl. He nodded to Chase. "Mr. Culver, I hope you're enjoying your stay."

"Well, it ain't Texas, but it's all right." Chase sure could lay it on thick when he wanted to.

"Yes, well, if there's anything I can do to make your time here more enjoyable…" He looked from Chase to Dana, his gaze curious. "Well, Dana, it doesn't seem you gave Mr. Culver much of a workout."

It was true. Normally they'd both be a bit red in the face, breathing hard, but since they'd spent most of their time sitting on the bench they hadn't even broken a sweat.

"She took pity on me today. Is there something you wanted?"

"Actually, I was hoping to have a word with Dana. If you two are done for the day." He looked expectantly at them, his dark eyes too keen.

"I'm meeting with another client in five minutes," Dana

said, avoiding Chase's eyes since she'd just told him her next appointment was in half an hour.

"I only need you for a couple of minutes." Kyle smiled that fake white smile of his. The guy was obsessed with whitening his teeth.

"I have to stop at the desk," Chase said, already on the move in that direction. "But I'd like to talk to you about our next appointment when you're done here."

"Fine. I'll be right there." She turned to Kyle, hoping he wanted to send her to security for questioning rather than ask her out yet again. "Yes?"

Kyle's gaze remained fixed on Chase's retreating back, a frown creasing his brows. He seemed to snap out of his trance and turned to Dana. "You're not going to believe this." He peeled back the right side of his suit coat, and for an insane moment she thought he was going to flash her. "Look," he said, trying discreetly to show her something in his inside breast pocket. "Guess what those are for."

She peered closer. Two Broadway tickets stuck out of his pocket. "Are those for—?"

"Yep."

"How did you get them?" The popular play had been sold out for months. She knew because she'd been trying to get tickets since before opening night.

"I have contacts."

"There's no way you could've—" She'd heard of scalpers getting a thousand dollars a ticket and even those were far and few between.

"They're for tonight. Seats ten rows from the stage." Looking smug, he adjusted his monogrammed French cuffs. "I thought we'd have dinner first. Or after the performance, if you'd like."

Galled that she was even the least bit tempted, her focus darted to Chase standing near Kelly's desk. This was probably her only chance in the world to see the play. And orchestra seats? Wow. The downside, of course, was that she'd have to go with Kyle. The thought made her shudder. No play was worth that.

Just then, Chase looked over at her. His mouth curved in a slow lazy smile and he winked before turning back to Kelly. She knew then that she was having dinner with him. How could she not?

"I'm sorry, Kyle. I can't go with you. But I appreciate you asking."

He reared his head back in surprise. "You're turning me down?"

"I have plans." She wanted to kick herself for elaborating, especially when she saw the growing anger in his eyes. The heck with him. The word *no* was all he needed or deserved. "Excuse me, please."

He took a step sideways, blocking her way. "Do you know how much trouble and expense I went through to get these tickets?"

She stiffened. "I'm sorry. Perhaps you should've asked me sooner. But I'm sure you'll enjoy the play."

His face darkened even more. Lowering his voice he said, "I got these for you."

"I don't know what else to say." When it looked as if he might reach for her arm, she quickly moved away. Certainly he wouldn't create a scene here in the lobby. But she wasn't taking any chances. He'd asked before, and she'd said no, but he'd never seemed this angry.

She almost didn't want to stop and talk to Chase. Instead, she thought seriously about heading for the ladies' room where she knew Kyle couldn't get to her. But then he could wait for her to come out.

As she approached Kelly and Chase, Kelly briefly locked eyes with her. Obviously her friend had seen the interchange with Kyle and was suspicious. Too bad a quick word with her was out of the question. Although Kelly would be taking a lunch break soon.

Resisting the urge to glance over her shoulder, Dana stopped at Kelly's desk anyway. "Am I interrupting?"

Chase smiled. "I'm always happy to see you, darlin'," he said, and Kelly's eyebrows lifted in amusement.

Dana ignored her teasing look. "You wanted to see me?" she asked in her professional, no-nonsense voice.

Challenge simmered in Chase's eyes. Darn him, he was going to mention dinner tonight. In front of Kelly. No, he wouldn't dare… Karma was on Dana's side because Kelly's phone rang. She excused herself and answered the call. Under the guise of being polite, they stepped away from her desk.

Without being obvious, Dana located Kyle. He was still in the lobby, near the entrance to the lounge. Appearing far too interested in what she was doing.

"Come on, Dana." Chase's gaze touching her lips was more like a caress. "Make my day."

"Dinner. At seven. I'll be here," she muttered, and then hurried toward the ladies' room.

DID SHE think she was too good for him? Did she have any idea how many people had been in line for this job at the St. Martine? All Ivy Leaguers. With pedigrees from old New England families. He'd aced them all out. Him, Kyle Williams from Pittsburgh, whose parents didn't have two dimes to rub together. Yet he'd pulled himself up from nothing, received a goddam Masters' degree from Cornell University.

Anger and frustration eating at his gut, Kyle watched Dana disappear into the women's washroom. She was a freaking farm girl herself. So what that she was built like a brick shithouse? The two girls who lived on the floor above him both had bodies that wouldn't quit. He'd bet either one of them would jump at the chance to go out with him.

Screw her.

Actually, that's exactly what he wanted to do. These tickets should've opened that door. He knew how badly she wanted to go see this play. And he knew he'd impressed her. He'd seen it in her eyes. Before she'd looked over at Culver.

Who the hell was he, anyway? There was something funny there. Not just between him and the Ice Princess. The guy didn't fit the part of a rich Texas businessman. Too rough around the edges. Poking around, asking so damn many questions. He didn't wear the right shoes or belt, or even the right kind of watch. Kyle knew because he'd done his homework. He'd studied those rich kids back in Cornell. And he'd heard their snide remarks about the wannabes.

That's what Culver was. He could be like any one of Kyle's high-school friends who got into bar fights over Monday-night football and ended up working in the steel mill with his pop. Not Kyle. He'd learned well. He knew how to get what he wanted.

And he wanted Dana. He'd sold his soul for these two tickets. She couldn't disrespect him like she had. No way he was going to stand for it.

7

"I HATE to say it, but we got nothin'." Gil Wagoner suited the St. Martine perfectly. Pushing sixty, tall, trim, with silver hair and golf tan making the head of security appear suave and distinguished, he even spoke the part. But as soon as the NYPD veteran found out that Chase was a fellow officer, he lost the facade and they got down to business.

"Except you gotta be thinkin' that it's an inside job." Chase had been hesitant about giving up his cover, but he'd talked to Gil for a good half hour before making the decision. He liked the guy, and besides, Chase quickly figured out brotherhood was going to get him further than rich hotel guest. This conversation was also going to save him a trip to the station. Gil would probably have as much useful information as the boys in blue did downtown.

"Oh, yeah. Gotta be. But whoever this guy is, he's good."

"So you think it's a man."

Gil laughed and scrubbed at his face. "I keep forgetting. It's a brand-new world out there. Equal opportunity and all that. Back in the day, nineteen out of twenty times the perp turned out to be male. Not anymore."

"Yep. That's the truth." Chase glanced around the small, cramped, windowless office. Four filing cabinets took up the far wall. Above them hung a couple of framed commendations from the department, but no medals. Not much to mark a twenty-one-year career. Good news for Chase. He didn't need some gung-ho ex-cop grilling him about his own scrape with IAD.

Almost as if Gil had read his mind, the older man narrowed his gaze, and over steepled fingers, stared at Chase. "Why did you say you're here? You can't be on the job."

Chase had already figured out how much he'd tell the man. And how much he wouldn't. "I'm here for a friend. He was one of your guests who got robbed."

Gil nodded slowly. "Your captain know you're here?"

"Nope."

"Took vacation?"

Chase smiled. "Something like that."

A knowing look entered Gil's eyes. "Hey, no problem. I got put on the bench a couple of times myself. Actually, it was my partner who jammed me up. But we both got suspended. Shit happens."

Chase didn't confirm or deny, he just nodded. If he had to give Gil a bigger bone to get information, he would, but he didn't like talking about that night two months ago. Apparently it didn't matter what he had to say, anyway. A review board would decide his fate. And he doubted the truth would have much to do with the outcome.

After too long a silence, Gil asked, "You work plainclothes?"

"Undercover."

Gil let out a low whistle. "Better you chase some hotel thief. Pays more money and safer."

Relieved he had an easy way to get back on track, Chase grinned. "You got that right, pal. So, I take it you couldn't lift any prints from the rooms that were hit?"

"Nope. No trace evidence. The thief's a damn ghost. And

before you ask, we have no returning guests the nights of the thefts. I checked."

Chase snorted. "That would be too easy. The boys downtown have any ideas?"

Gil's expression turned grim again. "First of all, I don't have to tell you this is low priority for them. None of the thefts have been big enough to warrant that much attention. Whoever the thief is, they know what they're doing, staying just below the mark." Gil shook his head. "The detective in charge likes one of the room-service waiters for it." He leaned across the desk, and, as if he thought someone could hear, he said, "I personally know that detective. He's a racist. The waiter is from Nigeria." Gil straightened again. "The kid didn't do it."

"Abrahim, right? He did work every night something went missing."

"Not the first time. He wasn't here. A sister or cousin was sick, or something. Since then he's worked every shift they'd give him for the money that he sends back home. So he's around a lot."

Taken aback, Chase got out his notebook. "The first theft being—"

"Two months ago. That's when it started."

That surprised the hell out of him. "I thought last month was the first."

"We're not gonna advertise."

"How many times have you been hit?"

"Five." Gil exhaled into his palm and then rubbed his jaw. "The hotel isn't liable, but they've been coughing up some hush money. This keeps up, no one's gonna want to stay at the St. Martine."

"What about the other hotels?"

"If anyone else got dealt into the game, they're keeping their mouths shut."

That sucked. They needed an exchange of information to narrow their leads. And if other hotels had problems it might also point to Dana. The mere thought left him cold. It didn't matter that he'd personally ruled her out, he had to question his objectivity. He also had to eliminate her. If not, she was still a suspect. He cleared his throat, hating like hell that he even had to ask the question. "There's this runner, Dana McGuire, who sometimes—"

"Yeah, I know Dana." The older man's face softened. "She's a good kid. She's not involved."

"Why?"

"She's not," he said, matter-of-factly. "Call it gut instinct."

"I got the same feeling, too," he said, and when Gil gave him a curious look, Chase added, "I've run a couple of times with her. She doesn't know who I am. I'm just another guest to her."

Gil nodded. "Yeah, she's only around here during the day, anyway. All the thefts either happened at night or early morning. We still have to talk to her. Kyle Williams, the new assistant manager, insists we interview everybody. Now that's a guy I'd like to see go down for this. You met him yet?"

Chase smiled. "Casually, but I know what you mean. You don't really think he's involved—"

"Probably not. Hard to be objective about that one though."

"You said he's new?"

"Started here about two months before the first theft, and yeah, I gave him some thought. But I don't think he's our man. Too bad."

Chase hesitated, but the question had to be asked. "What about your guys? They have access to the floors. They all solid?"

Gil knew the drill and didn't seem to take offense, just nodded gravely. "I hired every last one of them, and I was real careful screening them."

They continued to talk for the next fifteen minutes about which employees had been interviewed and which ones had the greatest opportunities and motive, and Chase was satisfied that Gil had been forthright about his investigation so far. Unfortunately, not much progress had been made.

To Chase's shame, his mind had started wandering, and he wasn't thinking half as much about the thefts as he was about having Dana come to his suite for dinner tonight. It was going to take all the willpower he possessed not to talk her into his bed, but it wouldn't be fair. Not now, not while he was still investigating for Roscoe and she hadn't been totally cleared.

Gil promised to keep his mouth shut about Chase and his cover, but still keep him in the loop. Likewise, Chase assured him he'd let him know about anything worthwhile he found out. He owed him that much, if only out of guilt for lying about his room being broken into.

He got up to leave and Gil said, "I heard that you didn't file a formal report about your break-in last night. I appreciate that. I don't need management crawling any farther up my ass."

"No problem. Nothing was taken." No way Chase was going to come clean on this one. After he'd poked around his room last night, he'd realized no one had broken in after all. He'd been the idiot who'd moved his briefcase and forgotten where he'd stashed the prop. But as soon as he realized what had happened, he saw the misunderstanding for what it was…the perfect opportunity to inject himself into the investigation without raising suspicion. Chase paused at the door. "I'll be in touch."

"One more thing." Gil smiled. "I'd watch myself, if I were you. For being one of the undercover guys, you slip back and forth to that cowboy thing too much."

DANA STARED at herself in the lobby bathroom mirror. She looked like the same woman from a week ago. Unless some alien being had taken over her human form, she had no excuse at all for acting so foolishly. Dinner again? In his suite this time? She might as well lay out the red carpet. What if he did anticipate more than dinner and some pleasant conversation?

Groaning, she bent over the sink and splashed her face with cold water. Good thing her so-called run with Chase had ended up being lightweight duty. Her second appointment ran her to the ground. The woman was preparing for the Chicago marathon in October and practically wanted to run to Brooklyn and back. Normally Dana would've welcomed the workout, but not today. Not when she was supposed to meet Chase for dinner in six hours.

Behind her she heard the bathroom door open and she pulled a paper towel from the dispenser and started blotting her face dry.

"Good, you're still here."

At the sound of Kelly's excited voice she turned around. "Something wrong?"

"No, I'm just—" Hovering at the door, she glanced over her shoulder, and then motioned for Dana to follow. "Come with me to the dungeon. I'm not supposed to be in the guest bathrooms."

Dana checked her watch. "I've got about fifteen minutes."

"That's more time than I have. Come on." Kelly held the door open just long enough for Dana to catch it, and then with a quick look toward the lobby, Kelly hurried around the corner to the employee door.

Dana followed her down the narrow hall, but instead of going to the cafeteria, Kelly ducked into the ladies' locker room with Dana right behind her. Since it was two hours before the day shift ended and the night shift began, the large room was quiet. Where the sinks and stalls were located at the back, someone hummed off-key, but whoever it was couldn't see them.

Kelly plopped down on one of the benches in front of the lockers, and Dana sat beside her. Her eyes wide and excited, Kelly asked, "What happened with Kyle?"

"What do you mean?"

"Earlier, in the lobby. What did he want to talk to you about?"

"What do you think?"

Kelly grinned. "He asked you out, and you sent one straight to the heart."

Dana sighed. "I wasn't trying to be nasty, but jeez, when is the guy going to get the hint?"

"Well, I'll tell you, girl, watch out because he is in one foul mood. He made Lindsey cry."

"You're kidding?" Dana had the urge to go punch him right in the nose. The new front-desk clerk was about as sweet and quiet as they came. "What a jerk." She looked more closely at Kelly. The area under her green eyes looked smudged, the skin a little dark. In fact, she seemed a bit drawn. "Were you crying? Did he—"

"No, no, of course not." She waved a dismissive hand. "That would be the day I'd let that little twerp get under my skin. I'm just tired. So where did he want to take you this time?"

"Somehow he got tickets for *Off the Mark* for tonight."

"Wow! Really?" Kelly frowned thoughtfully. "I thought those were impossible to get."

"I thought so, too."

"So how did he get them?"

"I don't know. I wasn't about to ask."

"Hmm. If he bought them off a scalper they had to have cost a small fortune." Kelly pursed her lips. "Makes you wonder."

Dana didn't ask what she meant. She knew because the same thought had crossed her mind. But she'd never say it out loud. That would be irresponsible. Besides, just because Kyle was a jerk, it didn't mean he was a thief.

The humming grew louder, and they both stayed silent until a woman in a kitchen uniform whom Dana didn't know passed them on her way out of the locker room.

Dana hoped she didn't hate herself for this, but… "Guess who I'm having dinner with tonight."

Kelly's lips turned up in amusement. "Gee, let me think about this. Would he be tall, dark, handsome and hails from Texas?"

Dana briefly closed her eyes. "Please tell me I'm not that obvious."

Kelly wrinkled her straight patrician nose. "Only to the discerning eye."

Dana slumped back. "Oh, great."

Kelly grinned. "Seriously, I don't think anyone noticed. Although…" Then she frowned. "Kyle asked an awful lot of questions about him after you both left. Not directed to me, but Lindsey."

"What kind of questions?"

Kelly shook her head. "I only caught a whiff. You'd have to ask her."

That would only make matters worse because she really didn't know Lindsey well. In fact, hardly at all. Anyway, Kyle's interest probably had more to do with Chase's room being broken into.

Kelly checked her watch and then stood. "If you want, I'll find out from Lindsey what's going on."

"No, it's okay, don't get involved."

"What do I care? I doubt I'll be here much longer." She walked over to a mirror near the door and fluffed out her curly strawberry-blond hair.

Dana's heart thudded. "You haven't made up your mind yet. You can't. After tonight I may have more news about Chase's film."

Kelly turned around and gave her a bittersweet look. "How many times have we been through this? Last year when they were casting for that new play with Peter Frechette we thought for sure this was it, our luck would change. Well, I did, anyway. You're smarter than I am. Calling it quits when you did." Kelly sighed wearily. "I can't keep doing this. It's always about what's going to happen next year and then I'll be happy. I'm so tired of it all."

The inevitable sank in. "You really are going home, aren't you?"

Kelly's eyes got suspiciously glassy. "I'm pretty sure at this point."

Dana's panic eased. *Pretty sure* was much better than *absolutely*. "What if this deal with Chase turns out to be a sure thing?" she asked, the uncertainty in Kelly's eyes all she needed. "Let's have lunch tomorrow. You, Amy and me. We'll talk more."

"How about the day after tomorrow? Amy has split days off this week so she'll be off and I will, too. That way we don't have to rush."

"I'll make sure I don't take an appointment." The timing was perfect. By then she should know more from Chase. Now all she had to do was get through tonight.

FOOLISHLY, Dana had been so nervous about dinner she hadn't realized the full scope of meeting Chase at the hotel at seven in the evening. Although she didn't know nearly as many of the night staff as the day crew, she recognized enough of them that if she weren't careful, rumors were sure to start. Especially with her wearing a short denim dress instead of her usual running clothes.

Fortunately, the lobby was crowded when she arrived. A group of nearly thirty Italian tourists milled around the front desk under the chandelier, blocking the entrance to the lobby lounge, straining to listen to their tour guide rattle off in Italian.

She slipped into the middle of the group and made her way toward the elevators. At least she knew she wouldn't run into Kyle. The play started in five minutes and with what he had to have spent on the tickets, she doubted he was going to blow them off. She hoped he'd found some other woman to focus his attention on. She'd given him enough hints to back off, now he was really starting to annoy her.

She had made it safely through the lobby and rounded the corner to the elevators when she saw Amy come out of the employee door. Dressed in jeans and a cute, red, off-the-shoulder top instead of her conservative burgundy uniform, her dark hair down and tousled—Dana almost didn't recognize her.

"Hey."

Amy looked startled. "Hey back."

Dana quickly pressed the elevator button, not wanting to linger out in the open. "What are you doing here on your day off?"

"I forgot something in my locker." Amy grinned. "I know why you're here."

"Jeez, thank you, Kelly."

"She mentioned it when she called to tell me about lunch."

Dana didn't care. She would've told Amy herself, and Kelly knew that. "I left you a message, too."

"Got it. I'm free all day."

The elevator doors slid open and Dana got inside, but kept the doors from closing. "Did Kelly seem excited when she told you about me meeting Chase?"

The puzzled frown on Amy's face said it all.

"Never mind. I'll talk to you later, okay? I'm trying to make myself scarce. I don't really want to be the subject of conversation in the cafeteria."

Amy nodded solemnly. "I hear you." The doors started to close, and she added, "Have fun."

Dana stood staring at the buttons for the different floors. Her thoughts raced in several directions, and melancholy settled over her like early-morning fog draped over her parents' farm. Just months ago Kelly and Amy would have been doing cartwheels over getting up close and personal with a real-honest-to-goodness film producer. No matter how slim the chance of being cast.

There would be no other topic of conversation. After every run with Chase, they'd be on her like white on rice, wanting to know every minute detail that was discussed. They'd play the what-if game over and over again until they made each other crazy. None of the old disappointments would matter, they'd be forgotten, at least for a while.

But not this time. The excitement and enthusiasm were dead.

Maybe that was the reason for Dana's own detour from the norm. She was in mourning. Because this was so not like her. What was it about Chase that had her doing such stupid things? This man lived on the other side of the country. There could be no emotional investment on her part. There certainly would be none on his. He had never once implied there would be, so why her thoughts even dared to go there was a joke.

Then there was the tension over the thefts. Security had to be working everyone over, judging by the staff's long faces.

The mood had clearly changed in the past couple of weeks. If anything, she should be staying as far away from the St. Martine as possible. Not stepping out of her normal routine by coming here for social reasons and giving them more cause to question her. It didn't matter that she had nothing to hide, she didn't need the hassle.

The doors opened, startling her. She hadn't left the lobby because she hadn't pushed the button to Chase's floor. Shaking her head, she took care of that, and the doors closed again. She sure hoped her mood improved. Or even better, maybe she should just have a quick drink with Chase and leave. Claim she didn't feel well.

Her cell phone rang and she automatically checked her watch as she flipped the phone open. She couldn't be that late. But it wasn't Chase. It was her mother.

For a split second she thought about not answering. But of course she had to. What if something was wrong? Receiving a call in the middle of the week was too odd.

"Hello?"

"Honey, I know you're busy. I'm glad I caught you."

"Mom? Is anything wrong?" She arrived at Chase's floor, got out of the elevator and leaned against the corridor wall, her pulse racing.

"No, no. Nothing. I've been thinking about you a lot, and I just wanted to hear your voice."

"So you're okay? Dad's okay?"

"We're both fine. And you?"

Dana knew exactly where her mother was sitting. In the ancient kitchen, at the butcher-block island, the phone cradled between her ear and shoulder, while she shelled peas and talked. The telltale clink of her gold wedding band hitting the bowl gave her away.

"I'm doing great, Mom. Busy."

Her mother laughed softly. "You're always busy," she said, and Dana flinched even though she knew her mother's remark hadn't been snide in the least.

That didn't ease the sting of shame for avoiding calls, or doling out the ones she made to them like a miser pinching his pennies.

"Anything exciting happening?" The latest euphemism for…*Are you up for any roles?*

Dana briefly closed her eyes. "The weather's been cooperating so I've been running a lot."

"Good. I need to get out more and get some exercise. I've been baking too much, trying to perfect my carrot cake for the fair in September." She chuckled nervously. "Honey, your father's birthday is next month, and I have most of my egg money from last year saved up, and I was thinking that if you could spare a few days…"

Oh, no. Dana briefly covered her mouth. She lowered her hand. "Mom, wait. You're not spending your egg money on plane fare for me." She bit her lower lip. "Anyway, I don't think I can come until Thanksgiving. I don't know what my schedule will look like." She cleared her throat. "You caught me at a weird time. I'm on my way to dinner with this producer. There may be something in the works—"

"Dana, that's wonderful."

"Thanksgiving, let's plan on that, okay? But I have to go."

They quickly said their goodbyes, and then Dana laid her head against the wall and sighed. What a day! And it wasn't over. She straightened, and saw Chase standing several yards away, holding an ice bucket.

8

"I WAS JUST getting some ice," Chase said lamely. Damn it, he knew he should've waited for her to arrive before he left the room. That was a conversation he had not wanted to overhear. "You look nice."

"Thanks," she said, looking miserable. "Listen, maybe we should—"

"Let's go inside." His room was near the elevator, and he took the key card out of his breast pocket and let them in.

Reluctance weighed in her steps as she crossed the threshold and stopped on the Oriental rug in the middle of the parlor.

He continued on to the wet bar against the mirrored wall to deposit the ice bucket, trying to think of something clever to say. "What would you like to drink? Unfortunately I didn't think to order some beer ahead of time, but the minibar is well stocked with everything else."

"I don't know that I'm staying."

He smiled. "Come on, darlin', let's just get everything out in the open and not let it ruin our evening."

Dana moistened her lush pink lips. "What exactly did you hear?"

"The part you probably didn't want me to."

"Terrific." She slid the strap of the small brown leather purse off her shoulder, and dropped the bag on a wing chair that faced the plush taupe-colored couch. "I'll have double anything. No, make that a triple."

Chase poured her a light gin and tonic, made himself a stronger one. If he had an ounce of good sense or decency, he would've let her get back on the elevator. Now that he knew the truth. She did have expectations that he could help her with a singing or acting career. She hadn't given up like she'd confided, and he was gonna end up bursting her bubble. He had to think fast. Find a way to let her down easy, but not blow his cover. This was definitely not one of his better days.

"Here you go." He handed her the drink. "How about we sit on the couch?"

"Does that window open?"

He turned toward the large plate of glass that framed a view of the city. "I doubt it. Too stuffy in here for you?"

"No." She took a big gulp. "But a leap sounds good right about now."

"Well, now, maybe I didn't hear everything, because what I did hear wasn't all that bad." He smiled. "Come here."

She didn't argue when he took her cold hand and led her to the couch. She set her glass down on the glass coffee table before lowering herself to the couch, keeping one hand on the hem of her dress. That didn't stop the denim from riding up to midthigh and making his heart start to gallop.

"Look," she said. "I lied to my mother. Or rather I misled her. That was about old stuff. You or your film had nothing to do with what I said."

He sat on the couch at a respectable distance from her, and thoughtfully sipped his drink. Maybe he wasn't in too much hot water. "You mind elaborating?"

She moistened her lips again, and he wasn't sure how much more he could take of her doing that. "I'm not here because

I want a role. I let my mother think that we had a business dinner because—" She looked down at her clasped hands. "Because that's what she wants to hear."

"Your parents don't know what you do?"

She slowly lifted her gaze to his. "They do and they don't. I mean, we don't exactly discuss the new path I've taken. They know fitness has always been important to me, but I doubt they regard it as a career."

"Ah. They think you're still in show business."

"Sort of." She grabbed her drink. "Yes."

Relief began to soak in. This really wasn't about her expecting him to make her a star. Other family stuff was going on. He of all people understood all that expectation crap. "How have you managed to pull that off?"

"Neither of them have ever been on a plane in their lives. If they drove here, I doubt they'd even get out of the car." Her lips curved in a bittersweet smile. "Mom would keep all the windows rolled up and the doors locked."

"Don't you go home to visit?" He winced at how critical he sounded. So did she. "I didn't mean anything by that. I'd be the last one to pass judgment. I haven't seen my folks in almost three years."

Curiosity slightly furrowed her brows as she studied him for a moment. "I make it back once a year, usually for Christmas, but I only stay for a couple of days, praying for a snowstorm. Nothing major. Just bad enough that no one will come calling." She threw in a self-deprecating laugh, her embarrassed gaze darting away.

"I'm sure everyone in town thinks I'm being a prima donna. Too good to visit my old friends, although fortunately the kids I hung out with in high school have mostly defected to Indianapolis or Chicago." She laid her head back, closed her eyes and groaned. "Next year is my ten-year class reunion."

Chase chuckled. "Maybe I should've made your gin and tonic a triple, after all."

That got a small smile out of her. She brought her head up and looked at him again. "If you're wondering why I've humiliated myself by telling you all this, it's only because it's the lesser of two evils."

"I figured. But you already made it clear you weren't interested in the business anymore." He watched closely for her reaction, but he got nothing. "Why don't you tell them the truth?"

She shifted, her body language broadcasting her unease. "I don't want to disappoint them. My parents, my teachers, my friends, everyone, they were so sure I'd… Look, it sounds silly, I know, even though we're close, some things we just don't talk about."

"Okay. Enough said."

"What about you? Why haven't you seen your parents?"

He knew that was coming. "My father and I still don't see eye-to-eye. Better we keep some geography between us."

"And your mother? You implied the other day you had a good relationship with her."

"We talk once a month, but she hasn't learned to stand up to him and that really sticks in my craw. You want another drink?" He got up before she answered. This was touchy ground. He wasn't looking for an exchange of confessions or encouraging words.

What his parents thought of him was their problem. He was a grown man. He didn't need their advice or approval, and he damn well didn't welcome their interference into his life. Worse, he didn't want them to find out he was being investigated by IAD. Wouldn't his father have a high time with that information?

Chase was a fool to take his father's contempt personally. He was a bitter man who hadn't made it past the eighth grade, and to hide his insecurity, he treated everyone close to him with scorn. The more his father came down on him, the more trouble he'd gotten into. Chase never had a chance of doing anything right in the man's eyes. He knew this now, but at the time, he hadn't been mature enough to see the situation for what it was, and the damage had been done.

He made it to the wet bar and realized he hadn't waited for her answer. Sliding a look at her glass, he saw that it was still half-full. "You hungry?"

She smiled. "Not yet."

He poured himself another drink, adding a splash more gin this time. He didn't like that look of understanding on her face. She may think she knew stuff about him, but she didn't. Only what he'd told her. And he'd been careful. His mother was the only human being on earth who knew about the mental scars left by the mighty Jeremiah, a legend in his own mind. Whether she chose to turn a blind eye to her husband's cruelty, or had wiped the pain from her memory, only she could say.

"Do you have brothers and sisters?"

Chase moved away from the bar, and to buy some thinking time, went to the window and glanced out at the stream of cars on the street below before returning to the couch. "Fortunately not."

Her eyebrows arched. She wore a little makeup, like the other night. Not too much. Mostly on her long, thick lashes. "Why do you say that?"

"I already told you. We weren't the picture-perfect family."

"No one's family is." She tilted her head to the side. "I've always wanted a brother or a sister. My parents would've both loved to have a whole houseful of kids. But Mom couldn't have any more children." She paused, wrinkling her nose. "Maybe that's why I'm so determined to make them happy. Or at least not disappoint them," she amended wryly. "We're all each other has, so the investment is greater. I've never thought about it before, but it makes sense."

He shrugged.

"Come on. You're an only child. What do you think?"

Was she gonna beat this issue to death? "Look, darlin', you and me, we come from different worlds."

"True, my parents didn't have money, but—"

"Whoa, I'm not talking about money."

At his curt tone, she blinked. Her gaze skittered to the Monet prints on the wall by the door, then nervously drifted to the Asian-style dining-room table, anywhere away from him. "This is really nice. I like taupe and mauve combinations."

"I didn't mean to bark at you." Which was exactly what he'd done. Barked like a common junkyard dog. What an idiot.

"It was me—" She shrugged sheepishly. "I like to analyze and dissect. I have a big mouth sometimes."

He had another description for her beautiful lush mouth. As if to taunt him, the tip of her tongue darted out and swiped at her lower lip. He slowly sipped his drink, and then said, "My family didn't have money when I was growing up. We ate well when the weather was good and the price of beef was up. Other times, I got real tired of canned beans and grits."

"Really?"

"Yeah." It was the truth. He felt he owed her that much. "Before and after school I worked my tail off around the place, which usually meant not a lot of time for studying. But if my grades slipped even the slightest, well, the gates of hell burst open. My old man would take it as a personal insult that he'd spawned a dummy. Got to the point where I didn't care if I passed or failed."

She reached over, put a hand on his knee and gave him a sympathetic smile. "Parents should be given a handbook when their kids are born."

Chase snorted. "Like that would've helped. You couldn't tell my pop a damn thing. He knew it all." He traced a finger across the petal-soft skin on the back of her hand. "Your folks did a good job. Bet they weren't given a handbook."

"Oh, yeah, right." She laughed. "I'm too much of a wimp to tell them I failed."

"I wouldn't call it failing. Sometimes we come to forks in the road and we have to reevaluate our choices." The conversation was getting dangerous. Not just because he'd already told her too much about himself, but because it had been too damn easy. A new experience that made him nervous. He'd only meant to comfort her about what she'd revealed. He never put the past out there like that. Or anything about himself. "We should order dinner."

He started to get up for the room-service menu, but she turned her hand over until their palms met, and lightly squeezed. He stopped, sinking back onto the couch beside her, but kept his gaze averted.

"Tell me about the forks you've come to," she said softly, keeping hold of his hand, her touch making him weak.

"I don't like dwelling on the past."

"No dwelling. I promise."

"What about the analyzing and dissecting?"

She laughed. "None of that, either."

He smiled. "I'm really not a touchy-feely kind of guy. Know what I mean?"

"No?" With mock horror, she quickly withdrew. "I'd better keep my hands to myself."

"For you, darlin', I'll make an exception. You can touch me anywhere you want."

"That is so big of you."

Chase bit back a laugh at the opening she'd handed him. He didn't want to embarrass her.

"I have a question."

He met her eyes. She looked too serious. He doubted he'd like what she was about to ask. "Go ahead."

"You mentioned you had a fiancée once…"

Why the hell had he opened that door? "Yes. Briefly."

"Well, now I'm curious." She twisted around so that she faced him, the top of her denim dress gaping and giving him a view of something pink and lacy.

He carefully kept his gaze on her face. "See here. This is what you'd call ironic because part of the reason Colleen and I didn't make it to the altar was because she claimed I wouldn't share enough of myself with her."

Dana's lips lifted in a skeptical smile. "Is that for real?"

He held up a hand. "It's the God's honest truth."

"Uh-huh. What's the other part?"

Ah, man. He hesitated, wondering if it was time to deviate from the truth. But this wasn't an undercover drug deal or an illegal arms ring he'd injected himself into. This was Dana, who'd trusted him enough to truly lay it all out a few minutes ago. "I wanted to be a cop. She didn't want to be a cop's wife."

"A cop?" She couldn't look more surprised if he'd told her he was running for president.

"Yep. I'd wanted to be a cop since I was ten. Everyone told

me I was crazy. Maybe that's what made the idea sound so appealing."

"What about your parents? They must've had major objections."

"My mother, of course, was worried. She didn't want to see me placed in harm's way. And Pop…" Amazing how after all these years the bitterness still had a way of digging in, like a knife, twisting and turning until the pain was all you could think about. "Well, he said it didn't matter what I wanted because no police force in the country would hire a worthless punk like me."

"Tell me he didn't say it like that."

"You don't know my old man."

"Stupid bastard." Dana pressed her lips together. "Sorry, I shouldn't have said that. He is your father."

"Sperm donor."

"Well, he had to eat his words because look how well you turned out."

Chase chuckled. If she only knew. Good thing she didn't, or he wouldn't be sitting here with her. "I was no angel as a kid. If there was trouble at school, I was the first one called to the principal's office. During my junior year, three girls had to cancel dates with me at the last minute when their parents found out I was the one picking them up."

She looked as if she didn't know if she should believe him or be worried.

He grinned. "You know how it is in a small town, you do one thing to get people riled and each time the story gets told, the tale gets taller and taller until it takes on a life of its own. And I tell you what, some of those older folks have the longest memories."

Dana's lips lifted in a token smile, while her mind seemed to be miles away. Who knew what she was thinking? Maybe why had she ever agreed to meet him for dinner? If she got up and left right now he wouldn't blame her. That's what the nice girls eventually did. They left.

"Have I gone and scared you off?"

"What? No. I was just thinking about what you said. We do have a lot in common."

He grinned. "You were the town's bad girl?"

"I was their golden girl. Same principle, different set of problems. You did what—" She stopped, frowned. "What did you do to get them 'riled?'"

"Well, you see, in Texas, football is not just a sport, it's a religion. Now mind you, I like watching the game myself, but those pompous-ass jocks had no sense of humor when it came to practical jokes."

Dana laughed. "I get the picture. You didn't mess with football or the team in our town, either. The games were the highlight of the week. I was a cheerleader. Head cheerleader. Did I totally mess up your opinion of me?"

"Totally."

She crossed one leg over the other, pink toenails peeking out from her strappy brown sandals, and gave his leg a playful nudge with the tips of her toes.

Now, how was he supposed to concentrate on their conversation? "Go back to what you were saying about being the golden girl."

She frowned thoughtfully for a moment as if weighing her answer. "I was the one who was expected to be the class valedictorian, the homecoming queen, the one who'd win the county-fair pageants, all that crazy stuff. I was held up to an impossible standard. Of course I didn't realize it at the time. Took me a while to figure it out. In fact, I think I'm just figuring it out now."

"Hey, at least you didn't wait until you were bouncing your grandkid on your knee."

"Oh, don't go there. I keep waiting for that question every time I talk to my mom."

"Having kids?"

She smiled. "I'm betting my parents are hoping for marriage first."

He nodded, still old-fashioned enough that he believed marriage should always come before children. "Valedictorian, huh?"

She rolled her eyes. "There were only eighty-two kids in my graduating class."

"Bet you were the prettiest valedictorian that school had ever had."

Glaring at him, she said, "I see you've nicely diverted the conversation away from yourself."

"Not intentionally, but that did turn out well."

Dana shook her head in mock disgust. "Fine. It doesn't matter, anyway. Whatever scrapes you had in the past, look what a success you've become."

He flinched, and then tried to mask his reaction with a shrug. So far, no one back home knew he'd been suspended. In fact, with the exception of his parents and two uncles, no one knew he was a cop. To the townspeople, with his long shaggy hair and torn jeans, riding the noisy motorcycle he used while undercover, he was the bad seed they'd always thought he was.

Admittedly, he got off on their faulty assumption. The smug bastards. But if his review went south and he got canned, they'd have been right about him all along. Screw them. What did he care what they thought? "Yeah, well, I've had my ups and downs," he said finally.

"We all have. We make mistakes. We learn. We move on. It's called progress, not perfection."

He smiled at her earnestness and unable to resist, dragged the back of his fingers down her smooth, satiny cheek. "Is that right?"

She leaned into his touch, her eyes briefly closing. "It is."

Damn, he wished he could see inside that pretty head of hers. Had she seriously given up on a show-business career, or did she see him as a ticket to a movie role? For selfish reasons, he wanted to believe she was done with the whole business. Practically speaking, that's what she'd told him. So if she'd lied and was secretly still interested, it wasn't on him.

"You look so serious," she said, turning her head so that her cheek rubbed against his hand. "What are you thinking?"

That he wanted to kiss her. Pick her up and carry her into the bedroom. Lay her across that big bed and then lock the door. "That we'd better order dinner." He got up and moved across the room without looking back.

9

UNEASY, Dana watched him pick up the leather-bound room-service menu. He kept his back to her longer than was necessary. Only moments ago she would've appreciated the view of his backside in those snug-fitting jeans. But his mood had obviously shifted, and she had no idea why. Did he think she was coming on to him? She had flirted, but so had he. In fact, last night, they'd done more than flirt. Had she said something wrong, or did he regret saying so much?

Torturing herself wasn't going to give her any answers, but she didn't want to ask him what was wrong, either. Maybe he didn't believe her explanation for what he'd overheard in the hall. Maybe he thought she was willing to sleep her way into a role.

Oh God.

"I should go," she said and abruptly stood.

He turned around then, not looking terribly surprised. Exhaling slowly, he said, "Maybe you should."

She nodded, unable to speak, her gaze frantically searching for her purse. Where the heck was it? She'd dropped it somewhere. Near the door maybe...

"Dana?"

"Where's my purse? I brought one." She checked the coffee table. "Didn't I bring a purse?"

"Dana."

"There it is." Relieved, she spotted it, nearly blending into the brown wing chair.

"I shouldn't have said that. It was stupid." He quickly crossed the room and cut her off. "I don't want you to go."

She dreaded meeting his eyes, but endured the inevitability with as much grace as possible. "It's okay. I knew I shouldn't have come."

A quiet desperation turned his eyes the gray of a winter storm, mesmerizing her with their intensity. He reached for her hands, and took them in his slightly roughened ones, squeezing a bit too tightly. "Please stay."

"I don't understand."

"The truth is, I'm not sure I do, either." He gently tugged her toward him.

She didn't have much choice. Her body seemed to act without her consent. She moved close enough to feel his warm breath on her cheek, feel the brush of his thigh across the front of hers.

He released her hands, and then bracketed her waist. "I like that dress on you."

"I like you in jeans and that polo shirt."

He smiled. "We'll call room service, order a nice dinner and take it from there."

She nodded slowly, totally unsure if staying was the right thing to do.

"But first I'm going to kiss you."

She drew in a deep breath. "You confuse me," she whispered.

One side of his mouth hiked up, and he slid his arms around her. "If you want to leave, no hard feelings."

She wanted him just to kiss her already. Quit talking, or she might change her mind and go. If she did, she'd have to distance herself from him. Even a business relationship would be difficult. The running part. Not his potential movie. She didn't care about an opportunity for herself, only for Kelly. Suffering the nerve-racking waiting and hoping would be like trying to beat an addiction all over again. She was in recovery from the madness. She was happy, content. Really.

She slid her arms around his neck and with their thighs pressed together, her belly flush against his, she could feel his arousal. Her nipples hardened and a slow burn sensitized her nerve endings. This wasn't going to be just one kiss. She knew it. He had to know it, too. She lifted her chin, and he took his time lowering his head, and then briefly touched his lips to hers before kissing the side of her jaw.

The path he forged back to her lips was sweet torture. He touched the tip of his tongue to the corner of her mouth, and as if he'd found the secret button, she opened for him. He swept his tongue inside, his exploration skillful and thorough. Any thought of leaving faded into oblivion. If he unbuttoned her dress, if he slid his hands beneath the hem, up her bare thighs, she wouldn't utter a single protest.

He molded his hands over the curve of her backside and then cupped the fleshiness through her denim dress, briefly deepening the kiss before pulling away. He looked down at her, restraint evident in the tenseness of his jaw, the cords running up the side of his neck, the flaring of his nostrils.

She stared, loathed to think how wanton she must look, but helpless to turn away. Should she retreat? Should she make the next move? Should she give him a cowardly sign that it was okay to cross the threshold?

"Time to order dinner," he said finally, his voice husky.

She slowly nodded because it was the right thing to do. His tone didn't imply that dinner was a suggestion. He had the good sense to call a time-out. Except he didn't release her.

He'd been sensible, now it was her turn. She lowered her arms to her sides and moved back. He hesitated, looking as if he'd reconsidered, and then with a deep sigh, turned and retrieved the room-service menu.

"Here," he said, handing it to her. "I think I have it memorized by now."

She accepted the leather folder with an unsteady hand. How on earth was she going to be able to eat now?

"Of course we could skip right to dessert," he said, and when she gave him a shocked look, he smiled. "They have three different kinds of cheesecake on the last page."

"What if cheesecake isn't what I had in mind?" she asked in her sexiest voice.

His brows went up. "Oh?"

"I may be more in the mood for ice cream," she said with a straight face.

"That sounds cold. Now whipped cream, there are a lot of things you can do with whipped cream."

"You're evil."

He laughed. "That's what they say."

She shivered and turned away, menu in hand. It wasn't what he'd said, but how he said it that threw her off balance. She couldn't keep going back and forth like this, engaging in this foreplay, and not make a decision on how she wanted this night to end.

She went back to the couch and sank down with the menu in her lap. When he picked up her empty glass and walked over to the bar to freshen her drink, she didn't say a word. Even though she didn't want more alcohol, the small reprieve was welcome. She tried to focus on the list of entrées, but her thoughts immediately went back to the whipped cream. Damn him.

Chase was taking his time at the bar, and with his back to her, she grabbed the opportunity to check out the fit of his jeans. They weren't new, but worn and snug and molded to a nice firm ass. For the first time she noticed that he wore cowboy boots that made him about two inches taller than his running shoes. She knew he already had to be over six feet, which was fine with her since in flats she was five-nine. Either way, kissing, hugging, they'd fitted together perfectly. She could only imagine how well they'd fit in bed.

"Ready?" He set her glass back down on the coffee table.

She blinked. "For what?"

"Do you know what you want for dinner?"

"Ah." She closed the menu. "I'll have the crab cakes."

"And?"

"That's it."

"Isn't that under appetizers?" Frowning, he took the menu from her.

"Yep. I'm saving room for dessert."

His gaze darted to her face. "And that would be?"

She smiled sweetly. "I thought the whipped cream sounded pretty good."

TALK ABOUT playing with fire. If Chase weren't careful, he was going to screw up this entire case. All because of a bright, beautiful, tall blonde with a sense of humor and honor that made him forget who he was and why he was here. Ironically, the only reason it occurred to him to watch his step was because Dana was safely out of sight, removed from temptation, hiding in the bathroom.

He held the door open for the room-service waiter as the man pushed the cart topped with their dirty dishes out of the room. Chase slipped the man an extra twenty for the speedy service. As soon as they'd finished eating, he'd called for the removal so they wouldn't be disturbed later.

After closing the door, he waited a couple of moments, and then looked out the peephole to make sure the waiter had left. Dana hadn't wanted to be seen in his room by a hotel employee and end up the topic of cafeteria conversation. Chase totally understood.

He knocked lightly at the bathroom door, his body beginning to thrum with excitement. He hadn't misread the signals. They were in for a long night. "The coast is clear."

She emerged, and he noticed that she'd touched up her lip gloss and brushed her long silky hair. "You must think I'm silly."

He was gonna have fun messing things up again. "I don't blame you for wanting your privacy." He backed into the parlor. "How about some music?"

"Sure. What kind of stuff do you listen to?"

"I'm from Texas, darlin'."

"Country?"

"Is there any other kind?"

"You're two miles from Broadway. I wouldn't say that too loudly."

"Is that what you sing? Show tunes?"

"Not my preference," she admitted. "But yes, of course. When I got here I learned quickly."

Chase motioned her to the couch while he fiddled with the stereo system for a moment, found a soft jazz station, and then joined her on the couch.

"That's not country."

He'd left just one lamp on, in the corner near the bedroom, so that only a soft glow lit the room. But damned if Dana's smile didn't light up the place as if there were a dozen lamps on.

"That's okay. Good mood music."

"Oh?" The teasing in her eyes made him feel as if he didn't have a care in the world. "What kind of mood are you trying to set?"

"You really want to know?" He slid his arm along the back of the seat.

She just smiled.

Chase laughed, picked up a lock of her hair and rubbed the silky strands between his fingers. Man, he must be getting old. Thirty-one and already over the hill, because for the first time in his life he wasn't in an all-fired-up hurry to get a woman into bed. He wanted just to look at her for a while, watch the way her eyes sparkled when she teased him, and simply enjoy the flawlessness of her skin. Even this close her face looked as if it'd been airbrushed like one of those models on the cover of a magazine.

He had so many questions he wanted to ask. Nothing to do with the case. Yeah, New York was loaded with beautiful women, but she was definitely a cut above the rest. Why hadn't someone else seen that? Why hadn't her career taken off? Plainly, she hadn't used her looks to parlay a role, but he bet she could've swung the vote in her favor a number of times. He liked that she wasn't the type to make that trade. Instead, she'd moved on, made another life for herself.

"You keep staring," she said finally, looking uneasy. "I know I don't have anything in my teeth because I checked."

He smiled, leisurely letting her hair curl around his finger. Admitting that he was wondering why she hadn't made it big probably wouldn't be his best move. "Just kicking back, enjoying the music, glad for your company."

The corners of her mouth twitched. "Even though I was one of those annoying cheerleaders."

He made a face. "Oh, man, did you have to remind me?"

Laughing, she bumped his arm with her shoulder, giving him another preview of pink lace. "I wasn't just a cheerleader, I was a darn good cheerleader."

"I bet you were. And I bet you dated the captain of the football team."

"Yes, I did. Josh wasn't some dumb jock, though. He was right behind me to be valedictorian. I think he plays for the Indianapolis Colts now."

"No kidding."

"Or maybe he's still with the Bears. I've kind of lost track."

"Any of your friends come here to see you?"

"In the beginning a couple of them did. Then they started getting married and having babies."

"Yeah, my friends, too. Half of them are either divorced now, or in the middle of a divorce. Looks like my partner might be getting back with his wife, though."

"Your partner?"

Chase felt the blood drain from his face. He shrugged. "I have my hands in a couple of other ventures. Sometimes I throw in with a partner."

"Really?" Politely interested, she tilted her head to the side. "What kind of ventures?"

"Nothing as exciting as the movie industry, I'm afraid."

"Tell me."

Yes, sir, this is what he got for taking his mind off business. For letting himself get distracted by a beautiful woman. He really was losing it. Maybe he deserved to get canned. The thought gave him pause. Had he been that careless two months ago? Is that why he'd ended up shot, and the biggest drug dealer in Dallas let off without so much as a slap on the wrist?

Restless suddenly, he got up. "You want some brandy?" he asked on the way to the wet bar. "Or there are a couple of other kinds of liqueurs here."

"No, thanks. I'm fine."

He took a snifter down from the glass shelf against the wall mirror and caught her reflection. She looked confused, jumpy even, as if she might leave at any moment. Naturally that would be best, but he didn't want that. He just had to keep his dumb mouth shut. Or use it for more pleasurable pursuits.

He poured himself half a snifter and then turned to her with an apologetic smile. "Not all of my ventures have panned out. Sorry for being touchy."

"Forget it. I think I know something about taking a gamble and it not panning out," she said in a self-deprecating tone. "We pick ourselves up and move on."

He got back to the couch, and put down the unwanted brandy. Oh, how he loved this woman's attitude. He held out a hand to her.

"What?"

"Trust me."

She eyed him with suspicion, but tentatively placed her hand in his. He pulled her to her feet, and guided them away from the coffee table, into the middle of the room.

"What are you doing?" she asked, her eyes narrowing.

He looped her arms around his neck, and then slid his around the lower part of her back, pulling her close enough that he could smell the soft floral scent in her hair.

She finally caught on. "We're going to dance?"

"We're going to try." He was officially out of his mind. He couldn't dance worth spit. Something about her made him want to know how. "This could get ugly."

She laughed softly. "What brought this on?"

They swayed in time to the music, not what anyone would call dancing, but it served the purpose. "It's the best excuse I knew to hold you."

Her eyes widened slightly, and then she lowered her lashes and whispered, "You don't need an excuse."

He slid his hands over the sweet curve of her backside and pulled her against his thickening cock. Not that she couldn't already have felt him straining against his fly. All evening he'd been in some form of arousal; hell, he'd been excited just knowing she was coming up to the suite.

She smelled so good. He closed his eyes and deeply inhaled the intoxicating aroma of vanilla and flowers, jasmine maybe, he wasn't sure. He moved his hands up her back, massaging lightly, pleased when she moaned softly.

"You feel so good," he murmured into her hair.

She snuggled against him, pressing her breasts into his chest. Her nipples were hard and ripe, and he wanted to see them so badly. Were they pink? Brown? Small? Large? He was going out of his mind.

She pulled away suddenly. "I think we should close the drapes."

It took him a second to work through the fog and process what she was saying. He followed her gaze out the window to the office building across the street. A few lights were on in some of the offices, but mostly it was dark. The hotel sat at an angle so that most of the view from the suite was part of the city skyline and even a wedge of Central Park. Although it would be difficult to see inside, it was possible.

"I see your point," he said and reluctantly released her. He went to the window and she followed, putting a hand on his arm when he was about to draw the drapes.

"I just wanted to have a look." She peered out the window

If offer card is missing, write to Harlequin Reader Service, 3010 Walden Ave., P.O. Box 1867, Buffalo, NY 14240-1867

NO POSTAGE
NECESSARY
IF MAILED
IN THE
UNITED STATES

BUSINESS REPLY MAIL

FIRST-CLASS MAIL   PERMIT NO. 717   BUFFALO, NY

POSTAGE WILL BE PAID BY ADDRESSEE

Harlequin Reader Service
3010 WALDEN AVENUE
PO BOX 1867
BUFFALO NY 14240-9952

Get FREE MERCHANDISE!

CROSSWORD GAME

Scratch the gold area on this Crossword Game to see what you're getting... *FREE!*

FREE BOOKS AND GIFTS

YES! *I WISH TO CLAIM MY FREE MERCHANDISE!*

I understand that my Free Merchandise consists of **TWO FREE BOOKS** and **TWO FREE MYSTERY GIFTS** (gifts are worth about $10) — and everything is mine to keep, with no purchase required, as explained on the back of this card.

351 HDL ESZE   151 HDL ESK3

FIRST NAME   LAST NAME

ADDRESS

APT. #   CITY

STATE/PROV.   ZIP/POSTAL CODE

Order online at:
www.try2free.com

▲ DETACH AND MAIL CARD TODAY! ▲

© 2008 HARLEQUIN ENTERPRISES LIMITED
® and ™ are trademarks owned and used by the trademark owner and/or its licensee.

(HX-B-09/08)

at the blaze of lights from the cars and buildings. "This city is amazing. Even at midnight there'll be just as many cars out as there are now. There's always something to do at every minute."

"You really do love it here."

"I wouldn't say that I love it. Not entirely. But I've learned to appreciate what it has to offer."

"Do you see yourself ever leaving?"

She stepped away so that he could draw the drapes. "Some day. Depending on how my new club does."

"Your new club?"

"A private workout place for personal trainers and their clients. I'm hoping to sign the lease and be able to open up for business in six months."

"Why not until then?"

"Money."

"Ah, that."

She smiled when he took her by the hand. "Yes, that one small pesky detail."

He pulled her into his arms again. The cop in him had questions about where she planned on getting this money, and if he were worth his salt he'd at least ask a few token ones. "Anticipating a windfall?"

"I wish. It'll take all my savings. Even then I've had to take on a partner. She's expecting some money soon and then she'll kick in half the cost."

Newfound money always piqued his interest. "Something like that doesn't sound as if it would require too much startup capital."

"The lease alone is a killer. So is top-of-the-line equipment."

"Is one of the gals from the hotel your partner?" he asked casually.

"Are you kidding? They don't have that kind of money,

either. One of my clients is waiting for her divorce settlement. Fortunately she'll be a silent partner so it won't be too bad."

His conscience was clear. No more questions. "I think that's enough talk," he said, pulling her closer.

"I believe you're right." She ran her palms up his chest and unfastened his top button.

10

DANA QUICKLY forgot that she'd sworn tonight would be nothing more than a quiet, platonic dinner. She'd be out of her mind to sleep with a client again, although she truly believed that Chase wasn't married. But still, this would be only a step above a one-night stand, something in which she totally didn't indulge.

No, this would be worse because Chase was a producer and even though she wasn't interested in a role, she was acting as a go-between for him and Kelly. And the truth was, if he had anything for Dana, she'd of course consider the possibility. Not that she'd rearrange her life in any way.

Chase ran his hands up and down her arms, his gaze roaming her face. "The drapes are already drawn in the bedroom."

She opened the door to it, but there was still time to stop this madness. Grab her purse. Give him a chaste kiss on the cheek. Say good-night.

Instead she nodded.

He kissed her, leisurely, his hands tightening around her arms, before releasing her and leading her into the bedroom. Hues of taupe and mauve were repeated in the king-size bed comforter and throw pillows in every shape and size. On the wall behind the bed, three black Chinese characters served as a nontraditional headboard.

"This is nice," she said.

His interest obviously far removed from the decor, Chase smiled and slipped the top button of her denim dress free. Since it was too awkward to reach the second button of his shirt, she went to work on his belt. He tightened his stomach muscles, inhaling sharply. Enjoying her newfound power, she brushed the back of her hand down his fly. He was already hard, and she shivered with anticipation.

He didn't waste any time after that. In seconds he had her dress unbuttoned to her waist, and skipping the rest, he pushed the denim over her shoulders. He stared at her lacy pink bra, tracing a finger over the scalloped edge, before unfastening the front hook. He parted the cups, his gaze fixed on her budded nipples.

She tried to yank his shirt hem from his jeans, but he wasn't finished with her. Gently, as if he thought she might break, he touched the tip of his forefinger to first one nipple and then the other. The touch was so light it was torturous.

She pressed against his hand, and he made a low, guttural sound before roughly pushing her bra straps and dress all the way off her shoulders.

He started to slide the dress down over her hips, but had to stop to unfasten another button before he could pull the denim low enough for her to step out of the dress. The bra fell to the floor behind her. His eyes darkening, he stepped back to look at her, standing in only a pink thong and strappy high-heeled sandals.

She'd never been self-conscious about her body, and she didn't care that he wanted to look, but she was impatient to do the same. She closed the distance between them and freed the hem of his shirt. He immediately lifted his arms and yanked the shirt off. His belt buckle was undone, but that was as far as she'd gotten.

Her gaze went to the ugly puckered red skin near his ribs, and she froze. "Oh my God."

He looked down at the scar. "You knew about that."

"Yes, but I didn't realize it was a—that it's—it looks like a gunshot wound. Uh, I've never seen one, but…"

"It is," he said grimly.

That admission prompted a whole new set of questions. "It looks recent," she said cautiously.

"Two months old."

"The other day you said it was an old injury."

He smiled wryly. "That's because I didn't think you'd see me without my shirt."

"Oh." She gingerly touched the skin around the wounded area. "This looks bad."

"It was at the time. It hurt like hell. Trust me, it's much better now."

"I saw your face when you grabbed that little boy. You were in pain."

"I'll admit that smarted." He unsnapped his jeans and unzipped his fly. "But I've recovered."

"How did it happen?"

"An accident."

She dragged her gaze away from the ugly red scarred tissue and met his guarded eyes. He obviously didn't want to elaborate. "I don't want to hurt you."

He smiled, and without breaking eye contact, kissed the back of her hand. "You won't hurt me."

"We have to be careful."

"Enough about that," he murmured as he lowered his head, and then laved her right nipple.

She stiffened and briefly closed her eyes, holding her breath until he'd finished with the other one.

"You'll have to tackle those," he said, indicating her sandals with a nod of his head. Then he sat at the edge of the bed and pulled off his cowboy boots.

It was both disconcerting and thrilling the way he couldn't seem to take his eyes off her. Made her clumsy and it took her two tries to get the darn sandals off. He rid himself of the jeans at the same time so that all that was left were his blue boxers. Very tented blue boxers.

"Come here," he said hoarsely, getting to his feet.

She took the two steps to get to him, and he grabbed hold of her hand and led her around to the side of the bed. He roughly pushed the throw pillows aside, half of them falling to the floor on the other side, and then he pulled back the comforter.

Dana made a move to crawl in, but he stopped her, framing her face with his hands and kissing her deeply. She put her palms against his smooth muscled chest, amazed that she'd actually started to tremble. Maybe because it had been so long since she'd been with a man, but more likely it was the intensity of his kiss that had her knees so weak she wasn't sure she could stand much longer.

She lowered her hands to the top of his boxers and felt his stomach muscles contract. She slid her fingers underneath his waistband, and he took his hands away from her face and found the elastic of her thong. Instead of pulling down her panties, he slid his hands around to her butt and filled his hands. She slid his boxers halfway down his hips, just low enough to free his hardened penis.

It nudged her bare belly and she wanted so badly to lean back for a look, but she contented herself with its heat pressed against her skin. Dampness spread between her thighs. He pulled her harder and harder against him until she could barely breathe. Finally, she forced her hand between their bodies and found the silken head already beaded with moisture.

At her touch, he moaned. He yanked the elastic waist from her thong over her hips and down her thighs. Before she could act, he got rid of his boxers. He turned her so that with gentle force, he laid her back on the bed, against the soft fluffy pillows, his biceps bunching with restraint. When he stood back, she finally got to look her fill. Her heart hammered her chest. He was worth the wait.

He muttered something under his breath.

"What's wrong?"

"Just a minute." He turned around and got his jeans, his back to her, his perfect firm backside making her pulse race erratically.

Then she saw it. On his side. "Chase, you have another scar."

"What?" He glanced at himself. "That's nothing. Over five years old."

The mark was long, as if he'd been slashed with a knife. "How did it happen?"

"No war stories. Not now. Okay?" He fished his wallet out of his pocket, withdrew a foil packet and headed back toward the bed, his gaze eating her alive and making her shiver with anticipation.

He was still hard, and she really didn't want to talk about his old wounds, either. Not now, anyway. He put the wrapped condom on the teak nightstand, and she started to scoot over to make room for him, but he blocked her movement with one hand braced on the bed. He bent his head and tasted her right breast, using his tongue to tease the puckered nipple.

She tried to lie still, but she couldn't. Her skin tingled with the awareness of what was to come. She reached for him, but he caught her hand and held it away while he continued to suckle her. She squirmed, forcing him to let her go. Forcing him to straighten.

He smiled at her, a slow feral smile as he crawled in beside her, stretching out so that their thighs and hips touched. Turning slightly toward her so that his cock lay heavy across her hipbone. "Okay," he said in a low husky whisper as he gently pushed the hair away from her face. "We'll play it your way."

She hadn't realized she had a plan. In fact, it had been so long since she'd been with a man, she hoped she remembered what to do. She'd had many opportunities, even here in Manhattan where women complained about the ineligibility of men all of the time, but she'd never been quick to jump into bed with someone. Maybe it was her midwestern sensibilities that warned her off meaningless affairs, or maybe it was because she'd found so few men appealing.

This was totally unlike her. But she didn't care. She just wanted to feel the silky hard length of him. Shifting so that she partially faced him, she swallowed when she felt his cock surge toward her navel. Her nipples grazed his chest, and he tensed, his hand fisting at his side. Only then did she realize he was trying not to touch her.

The discovery empowered her. Fueled her boldness, and she took a small nip at his chin. He promptly moved his head, inviting her kiss, but she ignored it and trailed her lips along his jaw and down the side of his neck where cords of muscle and veins popped with his struggle for self-control. She lingered only a moment and then moved down past his collarbone, dancing around the brown nub before she lowered her mouth to his ugly red scar.

With her tongue she laved and soothed the area around the wound before making her way down his ridged belly. His cock stood hard and proud, and she stopped to study the contrast of satiny smooth skin and rock-hardness. She touched her finger to the tip and swirled the moisture beaded there.

He sucked in an audible breath, and immediately the game changed. Chase grabbed her upper arm. "Darlin', you're moving way too fast."

She lifted her chin and hid a smile. "You don't like me touching you?"

"Too much." He raised himself, bracing his upper body on one elbow, and slid his hand between her thighs, and she nearly levitated off the bed, clamping her legs together like a vice. "You don't like me touching you?"

She laughed softly. "Jerk."

"I know." He moved his hand so that it was impossible for her to keep her thighs together.

Not that she wanted to keep him away. The promise alone of what was to come had her flushed and ready. She opened for him, closing her eyes as his fingers skimmed the nest of curls before dipping into that sweet moist spot that made her gasp for her next breath.

"Easy," he whispered. "We're gonna go nice and slow. Make it last a while."

She opened her eyes, and his lips curved in a slow, coaxing smile. He bowed his head and gently kissed her shoulder. The gesture was so sweet she relaxed. He moved to her collarbone and then swept his tongue across her left nipple. Distracted, she didn't realize he'd further parted her thighs. The next time he moved his head, he slid down between her legs so that his warm breath bathed her clit. With his firm pointed tongue, he touched her dead-on where it made her the craziest.

Afraid she'd totally come apart, she grabbed his head to keep him still. "I thought we were going to take it slow."

He ignored her for a moment, continuing to use his skillful

tongue. "This *is* slow," he said finally, pausing to kiss the inside of her thigh.

No, it wasn't. This was like step five. Something a good girl did after a dozen dates. Maybe. She didn't know for sure. She hadn't seen the same guy more than half a dozen times since high school. Sure, she'd dated Bobby all through junior year and then Josh the next year, but neither would've tried something like this, and she wouldn't have let him if they had. To her, this was the ultimate intimacy. The final frontier of trust.

"Chase?"

He looked at her, and something in her face or tone apparently sent him the message that she was uncomfortable because he immediately pulled himself up and stretched out beside her again.

"Okay." He kissed her lightly on the mouth, then pulled back right away, concern in his eyes.

She tasted herself on his lips and momentarily lost her mental balance. "Sorry," she murmured, and then got mad because she didn't have to apologize.

"I did something wrong." Chase leaned back and studied her face.

"No, you didn't. It's just that—" She grabbed the sheet and covered herself. This was horrible. She wasn't frigid, but that's what he had to think.

"You are so beautiful," he said, gently prying the sheet from her hands. "Let me look at you."

She didn't object. Just held her breath while he peeled back the sheet. The appreciation in his eyes helped melt some of her tension. She knew she had all the right stuff. She worked hard to stay fit and she was proud of her body. It was her middle-class, midwestern upbringing that she had trouble getting past. It was embarrassing, really, a modern woman living in Manhattan and not being sexually liberated or able to tell a man what she wanted.

Meeting her gaze, he flattened his palm on her belly. "We're not going to do anything you don't want to do."

"I didn't mean that I didn't— It's just—" Flustered, she groaned.

"It's okay." He kissed her hair.

He didn't understand, and she couldn't explain. She shifted so that his hand landed on her breast, and she reached for his cock, which wasn't so hard anymore. Her fault, but she'd remedy that. She stroked him slowly, and he closed his eyes, the awkward moment quickly passing. He teased her nipple between his thumb and finger, pinching a little too hard when she ran her palm firmly up his length, then lingered on the moist crown.

After the ridiculous display of cowardice, she had the crazy urge to put her mouth on him. She wouldn't, of course. It was only curiosity. Dangerous curiosity. Better saved for another time. If there was to be another time. Which she shouldn't be considering at this point. But maybe just one little taste…

As if he'd read her thoughts, he moaned, and moved against her palm. He'd gotten impressively hard in a matter of seconds, and the overwhelming desire to feel him inside of her, swelling, filling her with unimaginable pleasure threw her into a mental tailspin. She released him, and when he looked up in confusion, she kissed him, hard, deep, using the distraction to push him onto his back.

She smiled at how easily he gave in, immediately lying back against the pillows, his arms open in complete surrender. Inviting her exploration. Whatever she wanted to do to him, she doubted he'd object. But then he was a guy, and in her experience, there wasn't much off limits to that side of the species.

Dana kissed him again, briefly this time, her breasts grazing his chest, before moving her mouth down his slightly rough chin, to the base of his throat, to one hard brown nipple. A quick flick of her tongue and then she visited the other one, lingering a moment, enjoying the feel of her own nipple pressed against his hot penis. She moved her mouth back to his chin, carefully guiding his shaft through the valley between her breasts.

With a hiss, he brought his hands up and cupped her hips. She wasn't ready to give up control yet, and moved down, forcing him to release his grip as she trailed the tip of her tongue back down his chest to the swirl of hair around his belly button. His arms fell limply to his sides and his stomach muscles tensed.

She was wicked for teasing him like this, her mouth so close to his erection. Not just wicked, insane. She wasn't prepared to go any further with this exploration, although the fact that she was tempted shocked her. What spell had he cast on her? Who was this woman she was becoming?

She moved back up to his chest before she did something irrevocably foolish. Feeling awkward and inexperienced suddenly, she kissed him on the mouth and then stretched out beside him, her right breast nuzzling the side of his chest, her thigh touching his.

He smiled and then dipped his head to briefly lave her breast, resting his splayed hand casually on her belly. She tensed when he moved his hand lower, skimming the tight springy curls before slipping his hand between her thighs. She was wet and ready and despite suddenly tensing, he easily slid a finger inside her. With his thumb he found her clit, and seduced her with slow steady circles.

Dana whimpered and reflexively squeezed her thighs

together. He quickly withdrew, and a moment of panic seized her, but he wasn't getting up, only reaching for the condom he'd left on the nightstand. Swiftly he unwrapped it, and with her heart racing, she watched him roll the condom down his thick, hard cock.

He gently forced her legs apart and positioned himself between them. But instead of entering her, he spread her nether lips and again stroked her clit, slowly, his darkened eyes staying on her face. She clutched the sheets, pulling them loose when the pressure started to build.

"I want you inside of me," she pleaded. "Please."

"In a moment."

"Chase." She arched off the bed, biting down on her lower lip to keep from crying out too loud.

"That's a girl," he whispered hoarsely. "Let go."

"Please, Chase." She gasped when the first spasm hit. "Oh, my…"

He moved his hand and, lifting her hips, he plunged inside her. Another spasm gripped her and then another as he withdrew, only for a second. Quickly he pushed his way deeper inside her, igniting a fire that burned out of control as the spasms ravaged her body. Stifling a scream, she arched her back to meet his thrusts. The room seemed to spin, yet time stilled, She'd never wanted this as she did right now, with this man.

Chase groaned, and then cried out her name with a final plunge, filling her so completely that she collapsed in a boneless heap. He followed her down, his ragged breath warm and moist on the side of her neck. His lips touched her skin.

"Who knew, darlin'," he whispered, wrapping her tightly in his arms. "I'd find heaven in New York."

11

"HEY, sleepyhead."

Dana slowly opened her eyes. The room was dimly lit, only a faint glow coming through the open door. She blinked and turned toward the deep soothing, voice that had penetrated the haze of sleep.

Chase smiled at her, his teeth a flash of white in the semi-darkness. She tried to get up, but his arm around her tightened and she settled back onto his chest, the smattering of springy hair pressing into her cheek. She yawned, and quickly covered her mouth.

"I hated waking you." He kissed her hair.

"You didn't seem to mind the last two times." Still groggy, she vividly recalled how, exhausted, she'd drifted off to sleep and the amazing and creative way he'd used his mouth to get her attention.

"If you only knew how much restraint I just showed, you'd be so impressed."

She smiled, and because it was right there, she touched his nipple with the tip of her tongue.

He shuddered. "You're pushing your luck, darlin'."

"Yeah?"

"Yeah."

He moved so quickly she didn't have time to defend herself. He flipped her over and pinned her body down with his. One of his legs slid between hers. With a strangled laugh, she tried to twist away, but he'd captured both her wrists and held them above her head.

She lifted her head off the pillow, parting her lips for him. When he tried to kiss her, she bit his lower lip.

He sharply drew his head back. "So it's like that, is it?"

Dana grinned. "You started it."

"I did." He pushed her wrists closer together, so that he could hold them both with one hand.

"What are you—" She gasped when he slid his free hand between her thighs. She tried to squeeze them together, but his bent leg kept her spread. "I don't think I can do this," she said, already getting wet.

"You don't have to do anything," he told her, moving his mouth to her breasts.

She stiffened when he parted her lips and slid a finger inside her. With his thumb he lightly worked her clit. To her amazement, heat immediately suffused her body and she knew she was about to top her record of only an hour ago.

Already he knew her body too well. He found that spot of no return, and she twisted her hands free and fisted the sheets, knowing that later she'd need to find her way back home. The journey began with a gentle tug toward Neverland, before the waves claimed her, pulling her under until her vision blurred and time disappeared into a vortex.

Dana's hand began to cramp and she slowly released the bunched-up sheet. Her lids felt almost too heavy to lift, but she forced her eyes open. Chase was there, gazing down at her, and he smiled and then kissed the tip of her nose. He hadn't removed his hand from between her thighs, but he'd pulled back from that too-sensitive spot.

"You awake now?" he asked, smugness tugging at his mouth.

She swung her bent legs to the side, forcing him to withdraw his hand. "You're evil."

His eyebrows went up. "That's what you call it."

Smirking, she stroked him, finding him hard and ready.

"Oh, no." He covered her hand with his, but didn't immediately stop her. His eyes closed briefly and he moaned before slowly moving her hand away. "You won't be happy when I tell you what time it is."

His words effectively cooled her off. She got up on her elbows and strained to see the digital clock on the opposite nightstand.

"Oh, no. It can't be." She practically shoved him in her haste to crawl out of bed. The sheets tangled around her legs and she kicked impotently at them, but it was Chase who finally freed her. "I should have left an hour ago."

"The shift change isn't for another couple of hours. It should still be quiet downstairs."

She found her bra, but not her panties. She'd had every intention of leaving by two, three at the latest. "I know, but the housekeeping people are probably doing their final sweep of the public areas before they hand off to the day shift. Ah." She located her panties and stepped into them, wishing she'd had time for a shower.

"It's not against a hotel rule for you to be here, is it?" Chase got out of bed, too, but he was still semihard, and she had to turn away so she didn't embarrass herself by staring. "You're not an employee."

Jeez, it wasn't as if she hadn't had enough of him. But she really did have to go and she didn't know how strong she'd be if he made the slightest attempt to get her back into bed. "No, nothing like that." She slipped her bra on and fumbled with the hook. "It's the whole gossip thing."

"Too bad you didn't bring running clothes. You could've stayed for breakfast and then walked out like you'd just gotten here." He found her dress.

"I hadn't planned on—on this." She took the sorry-looking, wrinkled piece of denim from him. "Thanks."

He smiled, his gaze going to the front of her bra where her breasts mounded over the lacy pink cups. "I deserve a medal."

"Why?"

"Because I'm using every ounce of self-control not to drag you back to bed."

She quickly slid the dress over her head, and pulled it down over her hips. "Seriously. The doorman and luggage guy usually cover for each other and one of them manages to sneak in a nap, but he'll be up in about an hour." She fastened the top three buttons of her dress, tried to smooth out some of the wrinkles. "The night auditor has just finished taking his break so this is my last—" She stopped when she looked up and saw the grim expression on his face.

Would she make it worse by assuring him that she didn't usually do this? No doubt, that was exactly what he was thinking.

Finally, he smiled. "I won't keep you."

"See? Everybody knows everything that goes on here. I don't even work here and I hear things." She shrugged casually, and sickened by what he must think of her, she fled the bedroom under the pretense of looking for her purse.

"Dana. Wait."

She found the small bag on the wing chair in the parlor. She twisted the strap around her fingers, loathe to face him, even though she felt him behind her.

He put his hands on her shoulders and kissed the side of her neck. "I understand why you want to be careful. I come from a small town, too, remember?"

She smiled wryly. Was it really that simple? Slowly she turned to face him. "I know you think I'm silly." She glanced down. "You're still naked."

"I am."

"Not fair."

"Look, I don't think you're one bit silly, but if you wanna argue about it, I suggest we have dinner again tonight," he said, lowering his mouth to hers.

She thought she nodded, but she wasn't sure.

CHASE GOT out of the steamy hot shower and dried himself. He tucked the towel around his waist and checked his healing wound while he waited for the steam to clear from the bathroom mirror. Up close the fresh scar was red and unsightly. Bigger and uglier than a normal gunshot wound because he hadn't gotten it treated soon enough, and because Miguel Sanchez had shot him from only six feet away. Miraculously the bullet had missed his vital organs, but still, Chase was damn lucky to be alive.

Yeah, real lucky.

His career was probably in the toilet, and there was still a possibility he could go to prison. But he doubted that whoever the guys were in the department who had it in for him would go that far. Putting a cop inside…well, that was the same as murder. No, they'd never do it; humbling him, humiliating him, getting him off the force, that would be enough for them.

Hard as that was to take, seeing Sanchez go free was like taking another bullet. Right to the heart. The guy had already put millions of dollars in smack on the streets of Dallas. Schoolyards, teen dance clubs, parks, nothing was off limits to the scumbag. As long as his pockets were filled with cash, nothing mattered.

Ironically, the guy had a thirteen-year-old of his own. A sweet kid, who knew nothing of her father's filthy dealings. Chase knew because he'd spent a year undercover working his way into Sanchez's inner circle. A whole friggin' year of his life that hadn't amounted to even the smallest conviction.

Chase stared into the mirror, barely recognizing the man looking back. Anger distorted his face. Made the veins in his neck pop. That's the way it was every time he thought about Sanchez. Or of that night two months ago when everything went to hell. And damn if he could figure out what had gone wrong.

He'd played the part perfectly, said the right things, did what he was told, even when ordered to do things that made his stomach turn. In the end, Sanchez discovered Chase was a cop, there'd been a bloodbath and Sanchez had walked out unscathed. With all fingers pointing to Chase.

He'd gone over it in his head a hundred times and the only possible explanation was Carmen Rios and her big, sad, dark eyes. Still, it was hard to believe she had anything to do with outing him. How would she have known he was a cop? Yeah, he'd slept with her, but there'd been no pillow talk. He'd genuinely liked her…she was a decent woman who'd been overwhelmed by poverty and raising two kids on her own, and had gotten in over her head. She'd believed Sanchez's lies.

Chase briefly closed his eyes. She'd believed his lies, too. Now she was dead. It should've been Sanchez lying in the cold hard ground. Or even Chase. Not Carmen. Bad enough he had to live with what had happened, but now IAD was claiming everything that went down was because he couldn't keep his dick in his pants.

He stared grimly at his reflection. Was he being stupid again? This investigation was in no way the same caliber as the Sanchez sting. But had he compromised the case by sleeping with Dana? No, he was certain she had nothing to do with the thefts. Although the fact that she knew so much about the way the nightshift operated really bothered him. Surely there was a good explanation. As she'd said, the employees talked a lot in the cafeteria. Or maybe she'd done some homework before coming up to the suite.

She claimed she hadn't planned on staying the night, but she had to know something was gonna happen. A kindergartner could pick up on the chemistry between them.

Too bad that when she found out who he really was, she was gonna hate his guts. He wouldn't blame her. The thought still cut deep. If he explained everything to her now, maybe their budding relationship could be salvaged. Unfortunately, even if she weren't involved with the thefts, one of her friends could be.

He heard his cell phone ring and hurried out to the parlor where he'd left it on the bar. Before he answered he saw that it was Roscoe. Not the person he wanted to talk to.

"What did the police have to say?" Roscoe asked by way of greeting.

"It's probably an inside job."

Roscoe paused. "They said that?"

"Gil Wagoner is the head of hotel security. He was on the job for twenty-one years. From all the evidence—"

"I don't give a crap about what Wagoner says. If it's an inside job you don't think maybe he's in on it? I told you to talk to the police."

Chase didn't need this right now. The guy was a damn bulldozer. Didn't matter whether he knew what he was talking about or not. "Look, Roscoe—"

"If you're gun-shy about going to the station because of this mess down here, then you should've said something before I handed you the reins."

Chase gritted his teeth. "That has nothing to do with it. I saw the report the police took. They aren't going to give me anything more. To them this case is peanuts. Believe me, they aren't busting their asses to investigate."

Roscoe puffed on his cigar, the noise grating on Chase. "I'll say this once, that ring had better be back in my possession in time for the Heart Ball next Saturday. Mary Lou is cochair this year and she just might want to show the damn thing off."

"Hold it, we both know you're holding something back. Obviously that hinders my investigation. If I don't get anywhere, that's on you."

Roscoe let out a string of expletives.

"Look, Roscoe, you trusted me enough to look for the ring. You need to trust me with everything."

After a brief pause, Roscoe said, "I took the ring to New York to have a copy made. The why isn't important."

Insurance fraud. Had to be. But Chase was staying out of that one. "You didn't get the copy made, I take it."

"I told you all you need to know."

"I'm gonna make this real simple for you. I'm trying to find out who knew you had the ring. That's all I care about."

"I didn't make it to the jeweler," Roscoe said irritably. "No one knew I had the ring with me."

"Any particular reason you wanted to have the copy made in New York?"

Roscoe cursed. "Look, son, if anything I tell you gets out, I'll ruin you."

Chase snorted. "Stand in line."

Silence lengthened. "I wanted a copy so that I could auction off the original and Mary Lou wouldn't know about it. The auction house is there in New York."

Chase quickly processed the information. Things started to

make more sense. Obviously financial trouble was involved, and a man like Roscoe would escape that humiliation at all cost. "At any time did you ask about using the hotel safe?"

"No, I decided the ring would be safer in my room. How's that for irony?" He barked out a humorless laugh. "Understand that I'm not real particular how you get this ring back. You hear me?"

"Understood." Chase shook his head. "One more thing. Did you talk to anyone at the front desk or a doorman about directions to the jeweler or the auction house?"

"I don't know. Yeah, probably. Did you talk to the girl yet?"

"What girl?"

"The blonde. You know the one. She's a real looker. Dana."

Chase's gut tightened. "You had her on the list as a person who'd been in the hotel, but you hadn't had contact with."

"Yeah, that's right." He sounded edgy. Not good. "I think you should talk to her."

Chase felt as if the floor had buckled under his feet. Roscoe was the kind of guy who liked to flash his money and three-carat diamond pinkie ring to get a woman's attention. But not Dana. She wasn't the type to care about that kind of superficial stuff. In fact, a slob like Roscoe would make her run the other way. He hoped. "Something else you wanna tell me?"

"You know everything you need to."

"Roscoe."

"Call me tonight. Let me know what's going on."

"Roscoe, you can't—"

The call ended, and Chase threw the phone down with too much force. Cursing, he checked to make sure it still worked. What the hell was Dana's connection to Roscoe? Why had he singled her out? Obviously there was a reason—he just hoped like hell it wasn't the obvious one.

Feeling uneasy, he headed back to the bathroom where he'd left his clothes. He dropped the towel from around his waist and grabbed his boxers. As he pulled them up, he noticed a small reddish mark near his navel. A remnant of his night with Dana. He smiled, thinking about how shy she'd been when he tried to go down on her. She'd surprised him, but he kind of liked that she wasn't that experienced.

That further discounted the idea of her and Roscoe together. Downright ridiculous. Chase finished dressing, while replaying Roscoe's conversation in his head. The guy had singled Dana out for a reason. But damned if Chase could figure out why.

ELLEN laid down the pair of dumbbells, mopped her forehead and groaned. "I think I'm going to skip the treadmill today. I'm whipped."

"You know what they say, no pain, no gain." Dana glanced at the round clock on the brick wall of Ellen's basement exercise room. Privately, Dana had no problem with her client wanting to cut her session short. She welcomed the unexpected time off. Last night had worn her out. But in a good way. Chase had amazing stamina. She tried not to smile thinking about the hard time she'd give him the next time he wanted to bail on running.

"I have a good excuse. I had another late night with my soon-to-be ex." Ellen cocked her head to the side. "You, on the other hand, look as if you're walking on clouds. What's going on?"

"Why argue? Let the attorneys handle it." Dana turned to grab a towel. Mostly to avoid the curiosity in Ellen's eyes. The woman had become a casual friend, and in fact, would eventually become Dana's business partner when they opened the club, but that didn't mean Dana wanted to share anything as private as Chase with Ellen.

"I know, I know." Long dark hair clung to Ellen's moist cheeks and neck and she impatiently peeled away the strands and tucked them into her ponytail. "It makes me crazy every time I talk to him. I don't know why I keep listening to his stories."

Dana looked at her in alarm. "Does he want to move back in?"

"He says he does, and then the next week he changes his mind. Don't worry, though, that's not going to happen." Ellen's nervous gaze darted away, and she abruptly stood. "The house might be a problem."

"Oh, no." Dana knew how much the three-story brownstone meant to Ellen. She'd worked long and hard redoing the inside, preserving most of the original brick and adding new hardwood floors and incredibly detailed molding. "I thought he'd already agreed you could keep it."

"Well, now he's saying if I want to keep the house, I get no cash." Ellen's apologetic look told Dana all she needed to know. There'd be no partnership, which meant no club, because Dana sure as heck didn't have enough of her own money. "Like I said, don't worry. I'm not rolling over and playing dead on this. Our investments are worth more than the brownstone."

"What did your lawyer say?"

"I haven't told him yet. Listen, Dana, I shouldn't have told you, either. Don't look so discouraged. He's just shooting his mouth off. He wanted to stay over last night, and I said no freaking way. That's all. It doesn't mean anything."

Dana might have believed Ellen if she hadn't suddenly turned and headed for the small stainless-steel refrigerator tucked under the stairs that she kept stocked with water and juices. Ellen had trouble maintaining eye contact when she was nervous. If she got cornered in the divorce settlement, there was no way she'd give up the brownstone. Not that she blamed Ellen, but the situation still made Dana heartsick.

"Well, good thing we haven't signed a lease," she said breezily as she stuffed her towel into her black canvas gym bag. Of all the days not to have an appointment at the St. Martine. So what? She had extra time before she had another client scheduled. Maybe Kelly or Amy would be available with a shoulder to cry on. Not Chase, though. She didn't want to see him.

Yeah, right, who was she kidding?

Frowning, Ellen absently passed her a bottle of water. "That's supposed to happen soon, right?"

"Only to lock into the price Mr. Anderson quoted. But that's okay. We don't want to get trapped in a lease before you know where you stand financially."

Ellen nodded. "You're right."

Hearing the words, seeing the flicker of resignation in Ellen's eyes sealed Dana's disappointment. The thought that the club really might not become a reality struck like a ton of bricks. She had to get out of here. She didn't want Ellen to see how badly the news had affected her. It wasn't Ellen's fault their plans seemed to be falling apart. She'd been dealt enough grief with the divorce.

"Well, I'd better get moving." Dana kept her gaze lowered while she zipped her bag, and then gave Ellen a bright smile. "I still have a couple of more appointments to get to this afternoon."

"I'm really sorry, Dana."

"Don't give it a second thought. Really. You have enough to worry about."

"I still think we can make it work. Just not as soon as we'd planned."

Dana walked to the stairs, and paused to look at the detail in the railings, the antique brass light fixtures that Ellen had spent five months hunting down. "You concentrate on keeping this gorgeous house. The rest will fall into place."

Ellen smiled. "I'd hug you, but I'm sweating like a pig."

"Think I'll pass." Her stomach tied in knots, Dana hurried up the stairs and out of the brownstone because she really wasn't that good an actress.

12

AFTER Chase checked in with Gil and looked over the interviews with two room-service waiters and a maid who'd serviced the last two suites that had been robbed, he grabbed a quick lunch at a fast-food joint a couple of blocks from the hotel. Here he could sort his notes and make calls without worrying who might be looking over his shoulder.

Yeah, he could've stayed in the suite, but after last night, he'd had a hard time staying focused on the case. Everywhere he looked stirred a memory of Dana. Sitting on the couch with the hem of her denim dress riding up. Standing at the window looking out at the city lights, her lips sweetly parted. Lying in bed, her hair fanned across the pillow, her skin so flawless it made him ache.

Unfortunately, the phone call from Roscoe nipped at the heels of the good memories. What the hell was the connection between him and Dana? Obviously Chase couldn't ask her without inviting all sorts of questions he couldn't answer. He muttered a curse, and then smiled apologetically at the two small children with their mother, who glared at him from the next table.

He crumpled his wrappers as he got up and tossed them in the trash on his way out of the restaurant. He needed to talk to Kelly, who was supposed to be getting back from her lunch break about now. That left him a couple of hours before he'd meet Dana for dinner. To his amazement, the mere thought that he'd see her later started to make him hard.

Before he got out onto the sidewalk, he adjusted his jeans. Ridiculous how his body reacted like an adolescent's. There wasn't much he could do about the physical reaction, but he could force himself to stay on point.

That lasted about half a block to the hotel, because he saw Dana crossing the street. She wore white capris and a sleeve-less red blouse. Her pale hair was down, dusting her tan shoulders and shining like a beacon under the early-afternoon sun. Every man who passed her on the crosswalk turned for a second look. Even a couple of women eyed her. Not surprising. With her shoulders confidently pulled back, her perfect posture, her dancer's legs, she was probably often mistaken for a Broadway star. That's exactly where she belonged.

What the hell was wrong with these show-biz mucky mucks? Didn't they see what everyone else saw? Why hadn't they given her a chance, found a spot for her on stage? They'd broken her heart. And he was about to do it, too.

Spotting him just as she made it to his side of the street, she seemed surprised and not entirely pleased. For a moment, he thought she'd keep walking and not say anything. But she waited the few seconds it took for him to catch up to her. Guilt surged through him. Had she found him out? But then he saw the light pink spreading across her cheeks, and he recognized her reticence for what it was: shyness over their first meeting after last night.

Man, he wanted to touch her. The urge was so strong he jammed his hands into his pockets. "Hi."

"Hey." Her gaze took in his jeans and white cotton shirt. "I thought you had a meeting today."

"I did." Ah, now he understood her initial reaction to seeing him. That he had to lie didn't make him feel any better. "This morning."

"How did it go?" she asked casually, but there was nothing casual about the keen interest in her eyes.

"Hard to tell. You headed to the St. Martine?"

She nodded, and they continued walking shoulder to shoulder, parting only to sidestep the hordes of lunch-hour pedestrians coming from the other direction. "About tonight," she said softly.

"You aren't coming."

"I don't think it's a good idea." She kept looking straight ahead, refusing to make eye contact.

He passed a hand over his face, felt the stubble on his jaw. He purposely hadn't shaved, preferring to wait until this evening. "Did I do something wrong?"

"No." She swung a look at him. "No."

"My ugly scar freaked you out, huh?"

Her gaze slid down to his ribs. "I don't know that I want to be hanging around the hotel."

"The thefts?"

She nodded. "That, too."

He touched her arm. "What is it?"

She subtly moved away from him. "Last night was sloppy and risky and I know better. This might be a big city, but working in a hotel is like living in a small town."

"Someone saw you?"

"Just my friend from the front desk. At least she's the only one I know of."

"Amy? Did she work last night?"

Dana frowned at him. "She was picking something up from her locker."

"At five in the morning?"

"No, before I went up to your suite." Her frown turned to suspicion. "What's with the questions?"

He cleared his throat. "I'm trying to picture her. She's the dancer, right?"

Dana blinked, and then seemed to relax. "A very good one, too."

"But you're not biased."

She smiled. "Only slightly."

"Look, if you'd prefer to meet somewhere else for dinner, it's okay with me."

She moistened her lips. "Maybe that's a better idea," she said, but without enthusiasm.

"Or how about your place? I can pick up takeout and bring it over."

She looked at him as if he were out of his mind. "Oh, no. I live in a building that's older than dirt, and if you met my slob of a roommate I'd have to kill myself."

"Been there, done that."

"No, you don't understand."

He smiled, but let it drop. She thought he was rich—she was the one who didn't understand. But that's how it had to stay.

"Did you find out any more about who broke into your room?"

"I talked to security, but I don't think it's a priority for them since nothing was taken. Did you know there were five thefts all together?"

"I heard the number was in that neighborhood."

"You know most of the employees. What do you think?"

She slid him a resentful look. "I think you're wrong to assume it was one of them."

"You're being naive."

Anger glinted in her eyes. "Yes, I know a lot of the staff, but my opinion is based on the fact that most of these people have been with the St. Martine for decades. And most of the newer employees got their jobs because of the old-timers. They're hard-working, and frankly, they wouldn't risk losing a job at the St. Martine, because for many of them that's as good as it gets."

"Sounds like motive enough for me."

"Jeez, I can't imagine how cynical you'd be if you actually had something stolen."

She was right. He was sounding like a damn cop. "You're right. Bad day. That's my excuse. Probably because I'm sleep-deprived. Someone kept me up most of the night."

Her mouth opened in indignation, but she promptly closed it again as they approached the front of the St. Martine. One of the doormen tipped his hat to Dana and immediately opened the door for them. The older man seemed pleasant enough, but Chase knew when he was being sized up.

"You'll pay for that remark," she muttered under her breath, and then exchanged smiles with the bellman who passed them with a valet cart stacked high with designer luggage.

"I'm looking forward to it."

She lifted her chin, and he chuckled.

The lobby was loaded with tourists, cameras hanging from around their necks and brochures in their hands. Dana obviously didn't want to appear to be with him because without a word, she abruptly veered off toward the front desk.

That suited Chase fine. Since she hadn't said otherwise, he felt justified in assuming that she'd show up at his suite at seven as planned. He knew her at least well enough that she wouldn't stand him up. She might try to call later and cancel, but for now he was safe.

He headed for the elevators, resigned that now wasn't the time to talk to Kelly. In fact, he had a feeling that's where Dana was headed. He started really getting it that the three women were good friends and he'd have to be careful how he questioned Dana. Anyway, he had calls to make. Buddy would probably have an update for him, although Chase wasn't all that anxious to hear what those sneaky IAD bastards had to say. The final ruling was all that was gonna matter, period. Nah, he was more interested in asking his friend to use the department's computers and sneak in a couple of background checks for him.

Probably nothing, but he had a weird feeling about one of the room-service waiters, whose interview he'd read earlier. The guy hadn't consistently delivered to all the victims, but where he was assigned a delivery, he always seemed to take longer than necessary. Could be he was just lazy, but it was worth a look.

He got to the elevators, but paused to glance one last time in Dana's direction, where she'd stopped in front of Kelly's desk, one curvy hip leaning against the wall separating the front desk. The white fabric molded her perfect round backside, and he'd just bet she was wearing another thong. Her long legs were tan and fine, and he couldn't wait to have them wrapped around his waist again.

Stop. He had to stop. This was the kind of thing that got him in trouble. Tonight he'd see her. This afternoon he had to keep his mind on the job.

He swung his attention back to the elevator buttons, and literally had to step back to keep from bumping into the assistant manager. The guy had no regard for personal space.

"Mr. Culver…" The oily smile helped confirm Chase's first impression.

He didn't like the guy. Glancing at his name tag, he nodded. "Kyle."

"You're on the sixteenth floor, yes?" Kyle asked, and pressed the call button before Chase responded.

"You have a good memory," Chase said cordially, hoping like hell the weasel wasn't riding up with him. It wasn't because he knew Dana and Gil didn't like the man—Chase had a bad gut reaction to him from the beginning. He was rarely wrong. Except for Carmen.

"I'd like to think I take a special interest in all our guests." Kyle looked past Chase in the direction of the front desk. Or more pointedly, at Dana. He must have seen them walk in together. The guy was a complete joke. He couldn't possibly think he was in Dana's league.

Neither was Chase. She thought he was some big-shot rich producer. Not a broken cop. His mood went south so fast he didn't know how he was gonna make it to his room without totally blowing his cool.

"Did you want something, Kyle?" he asked with enough impatience that the guy had to take the hint.

"I want to make sure that we've responded to your—" He smiled at the older woman in the purple dress who'd come to wait beside them, except she had enough sense to give them room. "The incident the other night, I hope we've handled it to your satisfaction."

Right. "Yes, everything is fine."

Kyle eyed him with too much curiosity. The man was gonna be a problem. "Tell me, Mr. Culver, where is it that you're from again?"

To Chase's relief, the elevator dinged its arrival. He stepped back as the doors slid open, and then held the door for the woman. Ignoring Kyle, Chase followed her into the car.

Kyle entered right behind him and pressed the button for the sixteenth floor. The one for the tenth floor was already lit. Blessed silence descended until the elevator stopped. Once the woman got out, Kyle started in again.

"Where did you say you're from?"

Chase stared him in the eye. *Was this about Dana?* Or had Chase asked too many questions and made the man nervous. "Why?"

Kyle's phony smile faltered. "Your accent…it's interesting."

Chase gritted his teeth and watched the numbers flash above the door. Two more floors to go. "Texas."

"Dallas?"

The hair on the back of Chase's neck stood. *Had Kyle checked up on him?* "Look, what is this about?"

Kyle drew back, clearly not expecting Chase to take the offensive. The shorter man seemed at a momentary loss for words, which suited Chase just fine.

The elevator arrived at sixteen. The doors opened. If Kyle got off, too, Chase didn't know if he could stop himself from decking the twerp.

Chase started down the corridor toward his room. Maybe he'd have Buddy do a check on Kyle, as well. Wouldn't hurt his feelings if the guy turned out to be the thief. Picturing him in handcuffs made Chase smile.

"Mr. Culver?"

Chase stopped, grateful he'd put some distance between them. The guy didn't have an ounce of common sense, and the mood Chase was in, well, he was itching to rearrange someone's face. Slowly he turned to Kyle.

"If you need anything, I'll be around." Even the man's yellow tie annoyed Chase. "I'm making it a point to keep an eye on what goes on around here."

Chase knew damn well this was about Dana. "Too bad you didn't do that two nights ago."

WITH RELIEF, Dana watched Kyle get in the elevator. Too bad for Chase, but at least he was a guest and Kyle wouldn't be harassing him. She turned her attention back to Kelly, who was deep in conversation with a tall, dark-haired man, European-looking and vaguely familiar. Probably a guest Dana had seen in the lobby at some time. Except their conversation seemed more personal because Kelly, who never let guests rattle her, looked terribly upset. Enough that Dana thought twice about sticking around.

But she really wanted to talk to her about Ellen and the whole club thing. Not just to vent. Kelly was the one who'd hooked Dana up with her neighbor, Vinny, the man giving them the sweetheart deal on the lease. The trouble was, the place was going to be vacant and ready in six months even if Dana and Ellen weren't, and there was no way the man would let the place sit empty and unprofitable.

Really, there wasn't anything Kelly could do, and Dana absolutely didn't expect her to get involved, wouldn't allow it even if Kelly insisted, but she felt it was only fair to warn her friend that the deal might go south. She'd gone out of her way to arrange the meet and had pushed Vinny to give them a good price.

Kelly didn't look as if she were going to get rid of the clearly angry guest anytime soon, and she was getting more than a few curious looks from the rest of the staff. But abruptly the man jerked back, said something only Kelly could hear, and then stormed through the lobby.

Kelly sank into her chair, looking so shaken that Dana hesitated. She waited a moment for Kelly to collect herself, and then approached when it looked as if she were about to leave her desk. Kelly saw Dana and sat back down, her troubled gaze darting toward the front desk where the two clerks quickly looked away.

"You okay?" Dana asked, glancing over her shoulder to make sure that Kyle hadn't suddenly appeared.

"No." Kelly sighed, and then forced a shaky smile, her gaze leveled on Dana. "Did *everyone* in the lobby see that fiasco?"

No use lying. "Pretty much." She glanced at the two women behind the front desk who were both focused on their computers and then at the man at the adjoining bell desk. "But they're all back to work. He isn't a guest, is he?"

Kelly shook her head. "That's Eduardo, the guy I told you about that I've been seeing." She opened her top desk drawer, took out a bottle of aspirin and popped three into her mouth without water. "I told him not to show up when I'm working."

Well, now certainly wasn't the time to tell her about backing out on the deal with her neighbor. "Is there anything I can do?"

"You know a hit man?"

Dana smiled. "I forgot. Where did you meet him?"

Kelly waved an agitated hand. "At a club one night when I got off work," she muttered, glancing around, and then smiling briefly at something behind Dana.

Out of the corner of her eye, Dana saw two guests pass on their way to the elevator. When it was safe to speak again, Dana said, "None of my business, but I hope you're not going to see him again. That was not cool."

The uncertainty in Kelly's eyes was more than a bit disturbing. Surprising, too, because Kelly was normally a pretty tough cookie. "I told him this morning that I was thinking about going back home and that's why he went ballistic."

Dana's heart sank. She'd hoped that Kelly had given up on the idea of returning to Wisconsin. "Too bad. He had no right to act that way."

"I know," she said, obviously distracted. "Trust me, I did not find that acceptable. I don't want to talk about him anymore."

"So, you're really considering being a bank manager?"

"What?" Kelly frowned. "Oh. Look, I think I've attracted enough attention for one day. We'll talk later, okay?"

"Sure," Dana said apologetically. "I didn't mean to interrupt. I was hoping you had time for a break."

"Sorry, kiddo. I have to find theater tickets for that group that's taking over the fifth floor."

Dana had already moved back. "Are we still on for lunch tomorrow?"

Kelly nodded. "Annie's diner at twelve-thirty, right? I can't wait to hear about your date last night with—" She paused to make sure the front-desk girls weren't listening. "Tall, dark and you-know-who."

Dana rolled her eyes. Of course, Amy had told her about Chase. Which was fine, but that's as far as she wanted that kind of information to go. "I'll see you tomorrow then."

Deciding to hit the ladies' room before leaving, she turned toward the elevators. Standing just around the corner, not more than ten feet away, was Kyle. Judging by the way he glared at her, he'd just heard what Kelly said.

Great. Just great.

13

"HELLO, Kyle," she said pleasantly and tried to sidestep him.

"I'd like a word, if I may," he said, and blocked her path.

"I'm kind of in a hurry."

"This is important."

Dana didn't want to create a scene, but she had absolutely nothing to say to him and her patience was stretched thin enough today. "I have thirty seconds."

His long narrow face darkened, and she couldn't recall ever seeing him so angry. "You seem to be hanging around the St. Martine a lot lately."

She stiffened, knowing exactly where he was going with this. "No more than usual."

Challenge glinted in his eyes. "Not the best time to be changing your routine."

"What are you getting at?"

"I'm just saying that with all the—" He stopped, looked around, then moved horrifyingly closer. His cloying citrus cologne assaulted her nostrils and made her shudder. His gaze went to her neckline and lingered. "With the thefts and increasing police involvement, I would think you'd want to stay away as much as possible."

"If I were guilty, that might be true. But since I have nothing to hide—"

"The general manager is getting involved and leaning on security. He's insisting that the police take a more active role. I want to protect you. You know that, don't you?" he said in a hoarse whisper, moving close enough that his arm brushed the side of her breast.

She jerked away. "From what?" she snapped too loudly. Heads turned in their direction. She didn't care. "What are you implying?"

"Calm down." He moved back, pushing a manicured hand through his hair, a strained smile curving his mouth. "There is no implication."

"You're right. It sounded more like an accusation."

"No, no." He gave an emphatic shake of his head, looking genuinely distressed. "My only concern is that you not give the appearance of—let's say, impropriety."

Embarrassed and angry, she resisted the urge to look around and see if anyone had heard. Instead, she stared him in the eye. "You think I don't know what this is about?"

"I have no hidden agenda," he said slowly, guilt tightening his features and belying his words.

"You paid a lot of money for tickets last night, but I turned you down, and you're angry. Too bad. Get over it." This time she moved closer and lowered her voice to a bare whisper. "I will never go out with you, Kyle. Ever. Do yourself a favor and quit asking."

He opened his mouth to say something, but she hurried away while her shaky legs could still carry her. She hated confrontation and she hated having to be so brutally honest. But Kyle had asked for it.

She skipped the ladies' room, and hurried through the lobby as fast as she could without falling flat on her face. The doorman already had the door open for her and she didn't want to think about why he knew she was coming. She smiled a tight thanks and waited until she got out on the sidewalk to breathe.

Her heart pounded and her eyes blurred from anger. She didn't know Mr. Gallagher, the general manager, but she had every intention of making an appointment to see him. If complaining about Kyle ended up hurting her referrals from the hotel, so be it. Kyle wasn't fit to have a position in management. However, she wasn't sure she wanted to cause a commotion while Chase was still here.

Oh, damn.

Chase. Tonight.

Maybe that wasn't a good idea. Kyle was right about staying away from the hotel

After receiving several glares, she realized that she was standing in the middle of the sidewalk, disrupting foot traffic. She hurried to the corner and waited for the light to change, the idea of not seeing Chase tonight weighing heavy. In a few days, he'd be gone.

The thought made her stomach clench. The heck with Kyle. She wasn't doing anything wrong. And she sure as heck wasn't going to let him rob her of another night in heaven.

As soon as Chase got out of the shower, he checked his watch and then his cell phone. No messages. Good sign. A feeling of dread had settled like a murky fog over his afternoon. He'd been so sure Dana was going to cancel out on tonight, but since she was supposed to arrive in ten minutes, he figured he was safe.

He took his time dressing, examining the scar near his ribs, which unfortunately was still as red and ugly as last night. He hoped she didn't have any more questions about its origin. It was getting harder and harder to lie to her. But that was something he had to do, at least for another couple of days.

An hour ago he'd made some headway on the thefts by narrowing the suspect list. He'd discovered that the two room-service waiters he'd been looking at both had alibis for the night the ring went missing and had been eliminated as suspects. Turned out one of them had been on the schedule to work that night, but he'd left town at the last minute to attend a funeral somewhere upstate.

Chase really wished he could've eliminated Dana. He couldn't ignore the fact that she was on Roscoe's list, although now that he'd gotten to know her, he suspected her being there might have something to do with Roscoe's bruised ego. If he'd hit on her and she turned him down, Chase could see Roscoe holding a grudge and dragging her into the investigation. Nothing else made sense at this point. Still, he'd like to eliminate her once and for all. Part of the problem was he'd have to dig into her private life in order to do that, and he'd been reluctant to cross that line. Bad enough she was going to be furious when she found out who he was and what he'd been doing. He had confidence in Gil, and the man didn't think Dana was involved. Sloppy on Chase's part, but for now that was good enough for him.

One thing that disappointed him was not being able to nail that son of a bitch Kyle Williams. Of course the guy was still on his short list, but nothing would've given Chase more satisfaction than to collar the weasel. At least he hadn't been forced to rule him out. No matter what Gil had said.

Chase was still waiting for two phone calls to be returned, but he doubted he'd hear from anyone before tomorrow morning. Just as well because both of them pertained to Dana's friends, which would make it too awkward to talk with her sitting in the suite.

The knock at the door came just as he finished buttoning his shirt. His hair could use a combing, but at this length it was pretty hopeless no matter what he did. On his way to the door he tucked his shirt into his jeans. Mostly out of habit, he took a quick look through the peephole. Dana's hair was down and brushing a bare shoulder partially exposed under a pink T-shirt.

He opened the door, his pulse racing faster than it would the second before a major drug bust went down. She wasted no time rushing inside, forcing him to move out of her way. Pity it wasn't because she was anxious to see him. He knew she didn't want to be seen.

"Hi." She sounded breathless as she spun around to smile at him. "Sorry I nearly ran you over. I heard a room-service cart coming down the corridor."

"What?" He had to force himself to concentrate, to drag his gaze up to her face and keep it there. "Um, no problem." Her top wasn't a T-shirt, but was made of some type of clingy fabric that purposely slid off one shoulder and left nothing beneath to the imagination.

He swallowed hard. Twice. She wasn't wearing a bra.

"I know, I know." With an anguished look, she quickly hid his view by folding her arms across her chest. "I didn't know how bad it looked until I saw myself in the elevator mirror."

Chase laughed. "Honey, *bad* is not how I'd describe the way you look." All she had to do was glance down at his fly and she'd know… He pried her arms apart and at the risk of being a total pig, got another good look at the high jut of her breasts before taking one of her hands and pulling her close.

He slid his arms around her, and even through his shirt, he could feel her nipples hardening. Man, this wasn't good. He wanted to skip all the niceties, forget the foreplay and strip her naked. Lay her right down on the Oriental rug, spread her legs apart and sink inside her so deep she'd beg for mercy. Cry his name over and over as she came.

Hell, he really had to get a grip.

This was *not* good.

He put his mouth on hers, and she moved her hips, just enough so that her belly pressed against his already-hard cock. He found the seam of her lips, slightly parted, and plunged his tongue inside her mouth, withdrew and then plunged again, mimicking what he'd like to do between her thighs. She shivered in his arms.

He ran his hands down her back, over the sweet curve of her lush backside, cupping her and pulling her against him. Bad move. About to explode, he forced himself to slow down, to ease away from her tempting body. He abandoned her lips, but found that soft, sensitive spot below her ear. She let her head loll back, and he trailed his lips to her exposed collarbone, touching his tongue to the small hollow there.

"I hadn't planned on this," he whispered against her skin. "At least not until later."

She laughed softly. "I'm not complaining." Then she pushed against his mouth, arching her back slightly, offering him her breasts.

He hesitated, but only long enough to take her neckline between his teeth and test how far he could pull it down. Damn sexy top. He didn't want to ruin it. The fabric only came down to the middle of her bare breast, about two inches from her nipple. He used his hands to free the rosy crown, her flesh plumping above the neckline and begging for him to put his mouth on her.

Eager to please, he touched her with his tongue, only the tip, playing with her until she began to squirm. He smiled, and she slyly repaid him by running the back of her hand down his fly.

Chase groaned and involuntarily moved against her hand.

The woman knew how to fight back. But he wasn't done with her yet, and he lightly bit her nipple before drawing it into his mouth and suckling her until she whimpered. Then she laughed.

Not the reaction he expected. He brought his head up and looked at her. The strap of her purse had slid down her arm and she was adjusting it on her shoulder.

He smiled. "I guess I could've let you come in and settle down before I started behaving like a rutting bull."

"Yes, and I had absolutely nothing to do with any of this." Smiling back she adjusted her neckline, but the dampness from his mouth made the thin fabric cling to her nipple.

He had trouble looking away. "I could use a drink." He went straight for the bar before he mauled her all over again. "You want a drink?"

"Sure."

"I have beer."

"I'll take one." She dropped her purse on the same chair as last night. The sight took him aback because it seemed like a week since she'd been in this very room, a month since he'd seen her in the lobby for the first time. Three months. It didn't seem possible that he'd only known her for a matter of days.

He opened the small refrigerator, withdrew two bottles of the kind she'd ordered the other night in the restaurant and twisted off the caps.

"No glass for me." She sat on the couch, crossing those incredibly long legs of hers.

He joined her, a bottle for each of them in his hands. His body hadn't gotten back to normal yet, and when she noticed his state of semiarousal, she quickly shifted her attention. Made him smile. Sexy as she was and dressing as brazenly as she had, contradicted who she really was. A solid midwestern girl who was a tad shy and less sexually adventurous than most of her peers. He liked that about her. In fact, he couldn't think of a damn thing he didn't like.

She tipped the bottle, and he got hard again watching her enthusiastic mouth work the rim, moisture glistening on her lips.

"I needed this," she said once she'd lowered the bottle and laid her head back. "I hope you have a whole case."

"That bad a day, huh?"

"That bad."

"What happened?"

"You wouldn't be interested."

"Try me."

Without lifting her head, she turned and smiled at him. "I have to admit, I thought again about canceling, but I'm glad I'm here."

He noticed how much of the beer she'd chugged. Must have been a humdinger of a bad day. "I'm glad you're here, too. If you'd stood me up, I'd have cried like a baby."

She brought her head up then, chuckling. "That would have been worth seeing."

"Now, I know you're not that cruel, darlin'." He took her hand and kissed the back of it, and then intertwined their fingers. "Tell me what happened today."

She studied him for a moment, her gaze serious and assessing. "You really don't want to hear it."

"Wrong."

She sighed. "It's the club. The one I want to open in six months. Looks like my partner may not be able to come up with her share of the money in time for us to sign the lease."

"Ah."

She shrugged a shoulder, the bare one, and he had to work at keeping his mind on what she was saying. "I'm sure we'll find another place eventually, but not at that price."

It suddenly occurred to him that she might be hinting for him to offer financing. After all, she thought he had deep pockets. He'd hate that she'd expect something like that. No, his gut told him that wasn't in her nature…unless he was totally off his game when it came to her.

"I'm not asking you to fix things," she said, pulling her hand away and wrapping it around the bottle. "If that's what you're thinking."

"Hey…I didn't say a word."

"But you were thinking it."

"Well, I'll be damned. It's a crime to think in this city."

She took a gulp of beer. "That's the trouble with men…a woman can't just vent without them jumping in and designing a plan of action."

"Excuse me, darlin', but that's a mighty broad generalization."

"I'm just speaking from experience, that's all."

"You've been hanging out with the wrong kind of guys."

A reluctant smile tugged at her lips. "You have a point. Sorry. Didn't mean to jump down your throat."

"I will say that for some of us guys it's nice to play the hero, probably comes from knuckle-dragging for too long," he said, which sealed·the deal on her smile. "But I get that you're capable of taking care of your own problems." Something else occurred to him. "You seemed off when I saw you at the corner earlier. You must've just found out about your partner."

She nodded. "And then I went to let Kelly know about the snafu since she's the one who hooked us up with the man leasing us the space, and I ended up having a run-in with Kyle. He's the assistant manager here."

Chase's jaw tightened. "I know who he is. He rode the elevator up with me this afternoon."

She frowned. "Did he say something to you?"

"Nothing much."

"It was about me, wasn't it?"

Chase could see the tension in her face, and he took her hand again. "What's going on?"

She shook her head. "I think I burdened you with enough of my problems for one day."

"You're not getting off that easily."

Dana sighed. "Kyle is sour grapes over me refusing to go out with him and I'm pretty sure he knows about us." Her eyes widened slightly. "I mean, that we've seen each other socially. Oh, jeez, I hope that's all he knows."

"Even so, too bad. You're a big girl. Screw him."

"I think that's what he has in mind."

Surprised, Chase barked out a laugh.

"Bad joke. I know." She sagged dejectedly against the couch. "But he pointed out the lack of wisdom in hanging around the hotel more than usual at a time like this. And even though he has an ulterior motive for keeping me away, he's right."

Chase didn't say anything for a moment. Right or not, he sincerely wanted to smash the guy's face in. "He didn't imply you had anything to do with the thefts..."

"No way. I would've hurt him."

"Take a ticket, darlin'," he said, and she gave him a warning look. "Has security questioned you yet?"

"No, but it's a matter of time. I don't blame them for having to do it."

"Yeah. It's their job."

She briefly closed her eyes and groaned. "Maybe Kelly has the right idea about leaving. This city sucks."

Chase squeezed her hand. "She hasn't changed her mind, huh?"

"Not that she wouldn't," she said quickly, her gaze probing. "If the right opportunity presented itself."

He knew what she was getting at. Made him feel like dirt. Maybe now was the time to explain who he was. He knew Dana wasn't guilty. Every instinct convinced him, but he was still a cop, and she was still on the short list because he hadn't done his job and ruled her out. More importantly, her friends were on that list. That meant he had to keep his mouth shut. "You know I can't promise anything, right? It's too early."

"I know. I wasn't pushing." She withdrew again, shoving a frustrated hand through her hair. "I saw the man she's been dating in the lobby today. She told him she might be leaving and it wasn't pretty. Guess it finally sunk in for me that she's totally serious."

That got Chase's attention. "You know this guy?"

She shook her head. "She met him at a club about two months ago."

He knew the three women were tight. Odd that Kelly hadn't introduced them to the new man in her life. "What did he do in the lobby?"

"I mean, it wasn't like a huge scene or anything. He didn't yell, in fact I couldn't hear a word he said. But he upset Kelly big-time."

"What's this guy's name? I'll go take care of him for her."

Dana smiled. "I only know his first name, or maybe I'd take you up on the offer."

"That's enough. Tell me his first name."

She laughed, shaking her head at him.

Damn. It had been worth a shot. But asking her again for the man's name would only raise a red flag. Maybe the guy was nobody. A romantic interest, just like Kelly said. Or maybe he was her business partner who didn't like that he was about to lose his inside person. That would make him pretty irate.

"Hey." Dana tugged at his hand. "You look so serious. I'm sorry I unloaded on you."

"Nah, I was just thinking about this burglary business. I hate that they're going to question you."

"Oh, brother, that's the least of my worries."

"Still, it could end up being time-consuming." He drew the tip of his finger down her silky soft cheek and then brushed it across her lower lip. "And I have a vested interest on how you spend your free time this week."

A slow sexy smile curved her mouth. "Oh?"

"Yep." He leaned over and kissed her briefly so he wouldn't mess up and take her straight to bed. "So this is what we're going to do. I'm going to call room service and order our dinner and then—"

"We could skip dinner," she said, stroking his thigh.

He would *not* let her distract him. "No, because while we're waiting for our food, we're going to go over your alibis."

She blinked, and then stared at him as if he'd asked her to run down Fifth Avenue topless. "Why?"

"When security asks, will you know where you were on the nights the thefts occurred?"

"I don't know. Maybe." She drained the last of her beer, her brows drawn together in a worried frown. "This is crazy. I don't have anything to hide."

"I know. Let's make sure security and the police know that, too."

Her frown deepening, she murmured, "Good point.
should be prepared."

Nodding, he got up, anxious to dial room service. This wa
perfect. He could cross her off the list. "Know what you want?

"The salmon," she said absently, staring off into space.

Good. The sooner he could eliminate her the better. H
gave their order, impatient when he had to repeat his wine se
lection, and then he rejoined her on the couch.

"Okay," he said, "let's start from the beginning."

She gave him a seductive smile. "You're nice to be con
cerned, but I hate wasting time on that tonight." She move
closer. "Not when there's so many better things to do."

Her lips touched his, and fool that he was, that's all it too
to forget everything but the hope of burying himself in he
sweet, wet softness.

14

IF SHE had to hide out, this was the place to do it. With a whirl-pool bath and separate shower, the suite's bathroom was almost as big as Dana's bedroom. She ran her palm over the glossy blue-pearl granite counter and listened to the clang of silver as the room-service waitress removed their dinner dishes. It seemed so juvenile, and she really shouldn't care if the staff knew she was seeing a guest. But telling herself that and not fretting about the hotel grapevine were two different things.

She looked at herself in the mirror and gasped at her clingy pink top. Good grief. She plucked at the fabric, damp from Chase's mouth and molding her breast like a second skin. The outline of her nipple was so obvious she might as well be wearing nothing. She wasn't all that big-chested and she often didn't wear a bra, but with this kind of material…well, bad idea.

The fact that it was damp didn't help. She noticed the blow dryer hanging on the wall and figured she could take care of that in just a couple of minutes. She got the dryer down, turned it on and aimed the nozzle at her shirt. The air got hot in a hurry and she reduced the amount of heat. That's when she heard the knock at the door, and turned off the dryer.

"Chase?"

"She's gone."

She eyed the offending spot, only marginally improved,

and replaced the dryer on the wall hook. She opened the door
prepared to leave the bathroom, but Chase blocked her way

He smiled, and moved forward so that she was forced to
back into the bathroom.

"What?" she asked with a nervous laugh.

Saying nothing, he took the hem of her shirt and pulled it
up over her head. He tossed it onto the counter, his darken
ing eyes never leaving her face. "I want you," he whispered

"I want you, too," she said, her voice barely audible.

The dampness already beginning to pool between her
thighs, she unbuttoned his white shirt. Before she could get
to it, he yanked the tails from the waistband of his jeans, and
then shrugged out of it, letting it fall in a heap on the black
and-gray tile floor.

He broke eye contact then, lowering his appreciative gaze
to her breasts, his nostrils flaring slightly. He touched the tip
of one nipple, fingering the tight, aching bud before putting
his mouth on her. She closed her eyes and wove her fingers
through his hair, enjoying the pleasant warmth that blossomed
in her belly and then traveled south. Moments later, she felt
his hand on her zipper.

She reached for his snap and for a few seconds their arms
became entangled. They laughed, and then in a heated frenzy
finally rid each other of their jeans, leaving him in white boxers
and her in a pink thong. Her gaze immediately went to the scar
near his ribs. He obviously hadn't taken care of the wound and
that's why it had healed so badly. That alone made her curious

He followed her gaze and flinched when he saw the scar
almost as if he'd forgotten it was there. "Yeah, I know. What
a turn-off."

"No, no." She gave his arm a gentle shove. "I hurt for you
that's all."

He stared into her eyes, his brows furrowed, almost as if he didn't believe her. "Trust me. I don't deserve your sympathy."

"Tough. You've got it."

One side of his mouth hiked up, and with his eyes still fastened on hers, he inclined his head toward the whirlpool bath. "Sure would be a shame to waste that tub."

"Funny, I was thinking the same thing."

"Were you now?" he asked, intertwining his fingers with the elastic of her thong.

She smiled slowly. "You bet, cowboy."

He was so quick she barely realized that he'd slid her thong down her thighs. She took it from there, yanking the scrap of silk over her calves and then kicking it off. It landed in one of the sinks, and they dissolved into laughter again.

This was crazy. She didn't know why she was so giddy. She'd had only one beer and two glasses of wine, and that had been over a two-hour period. Maybe that was it. She wasn't used to drinking wine, and the few times she had, she'd felt the effect quite easily. Mostly though, she was just too comfortable with Chase. He was so darn easy to talk to that it was almost scary. Not almost. It *was* scary. She hated the thought that he'd be gone in a few days.

No, she couldn't allow herself to start thinking about him leaving. That would totally ruin tonight. She knew before going into this tryst that it would be short-term. Unless, of course, he ended up financing a film project and then—

She ruthlessly stopped herself. She wasn't after a job. And she certainly wasn't after a relationship. But she was after those boxers.

With a sly smile, she grabbed hold of the waistband and yanked the elastic down. He wasn't shy about taking over. In a split second he was naked, his penis already thick and heavy against her bare skin as he pulled her into his arms and kissed the side of her neck.

"Let's get the water started," she said, briefly closing her eyes, her skin starting to get all tingly, and for an instant she wondered if it was worth waiting for the tub to fill up.

"On it," he murmured, and trailed his mouth down to her breasts as he reached for the faucet behind her.

She flattened her palm against the wall to maintain balance when her knees weakened. He managed to start the water without once breaking contact, his hand warm on her flesh.

When he stood again, he pulled her closer, capturing her mouth in a kiss that made her even more unsteady. He thrust his tongue inside possessively as he pressed his erection against her hip.

She gave as good as she got. With one hand holding his shoulder, the other snaked down between them until her fingers found his cock. She dipped into the pearl of moisture at the tip then traced the crown, feeling his excitement in his indrawn breath, in the way he nipped the side of her mouth then plunged inside her once more.

She wanted him closer, wanted to feel every part of him. The sound of the water rushing into the tub seemed a perfect soundtrack. Crashing, filling, rushing with the same ferocious rhythm as her heartbeat.

Chase clearly wanted the same thing. He ran his hands down her back, cupping her ass for a hard squeeze before he lifted her a good inch. When he put her back down, he slipped his knee between her legs then up so it rubbed against her aching sex.

His hiss as he threw his head back confused her for a second, until she realized she'd squeezed him a little too hard in her enthusiasm. While she eased up, she didn't release him.

Instead, she moved her hand down, gently, until she cupped his balls. This made him hiss again, only this time it wasn't because she'd hurt him. At least not in a bad way.

He was so hot. As if he was burning up. Dana knew her own skin must be just as fevered. As if she was blushing everywhere.

He looked at her through half-closed eyes, and his smile held all kinds of wicked promise. Then he captured her hands and pulled them up as he pushed her back against the wall.

Dana jerked at the contact with the wall, but in seconds the cool surface warmed. He lifted her hands until they were level with her head.

"Don't move."

Mesmerized, she nodded.

He let her go and walked to the sink where he pulled out a drawer.

She didn't move a muscle. Except for her gaze, which was drawn to him, to his long back, his extraordinarily fine ass, the legs that were at once long, lean and strong. So intent was she that she didn't think about what he was doing, only what staring at him did to her insides.

She had to squeeze her legs together, trying to control the ache of wanting him. Her hands curled into tight fists as he turned. Of course, she had no choice but to look at his erection.

She'd always appreciated a nice-looking man, but Chase was off the charts. Every part of him appealed, from his chiseled chest to his slim hips. Even his scar was sexy to her and she thought briefly about what it would feel like under her tongue.

Her gaze never left him as he went to the tub to shut off the water, as he pressed the buttons to activate the jets.

Then he was back, standing in front of her, close enough for her to see the intent in his eyes, but not touching her.

Still, she didn't move her hands from where he'd placed

them. It was impossibly hard to keep herself steady as she watched him tear open a condom wrapper. Each breath became a struggle as she waited for him to roll the condom over his erection, the anticipation building to the bursting point.

His smile told her to hang tight, that this was going to be one hell of a ride. She bit down on her lower lip as her eyes closed, waiting for him to pull her close.

Only, he didn't.

She felt his hands on her sides, felt him move down. Surprised, she had to look, to see that he was sliding down her body in slow motion.

He flicked her right nipple on his way, kissed her belly a dozen times until he knelt in front of her. Of course she realized what he wanted to do, and for a moment, knots came to her stomach and her throat.

He looked up at her, his hands gentle on her hips. "I want to taste you," he said, his voice barely audible over the sound of the watery jets. "I want to give you pleasure, and feel you come on my tongue. I want you to love this, to lose control. But if it's not what you want, then it's not what I want."

She stared into his eyes, into the need that was so clear. Her thoughts were a jumble of what had always been and what could be, but in the end, her body decided for her.

Her arms came down to rest on his shoulders as her legs parted. It was the most natural, easiest move in the world. Opening herself to him. Giving herself permission not just to trust, but to enjoy, to wallow in the pleasure he offered her.

He smiled just before he kissed the top of her mound. Then he leaned back to catch her gaze once more. "Thank you," he whispered.

She didn't even hear him. Instead, she read not only his lips, but his earnestness. Then he kissed her again, lower.

Steady against the cool wall, she closed her eyes, abandoning herself to whatever he would do.

She felt his breath on her lips, but only for a second. The moist pressure of his tongue followed, lapping at the crease as if she were a lollipop. The image made her smile, but the second his tongue sneaked between her lips, the image shifted into one not nearly so lyrical.

Although she could have opened her eyes and watched him with his mouth on her, she saw him through her mind's eye, as if she were standing outside her own body, an observer to this incredibly intimate scene.

She let her gaze run down his back, tracing his muscles and how they bunched and released. She could see the bottom of his feet and that felt oddly naughty, as if she were stealing a forbidden glance.

As Chase moved his hands from her hips to between her legs, she held her breath, not quite clear what his intention was. Then his thumbs spread her lips apart, and now his breath was warm where no breath had been before.

Still with her eyes closed tight, with her breath coming in small, quick gasps, she pictured him leaning forward, touching her clit with the tip of his tongue, and her whole body shivered, not just from the feel of him, but from the incredibly erotic images dancing in her head.

It was as if she was experiencing everything twice—his real tongue, warm, wet, circling as the pressure increased, and as the voyeur, the mere sight of his licking her bringing her alarmingly close to orgasm.

The sensations hit her everywhere. In her stomach, her chest. She felt lightheaded and breathless. She had to hold him tightly as her knees grew weak.

Chase moaned as he licked her, as he thrust into her with

that amazing tongue, and hearing him made everything even more intense. He was moaning with pleasure, moaning because he was doing this to her, and she was moaning back because it felt so incredible, so indescribable.

Her fingers clutched his shoulders as her hips rocked. There was no choice involved, her body was moving on its own, pushing against him, greedy for more.

He, in turn, held tightly to her ass, forcing her to stop, forcing the pressure to come only from the circling tip of his tongue applied in that one spot.

Her mouth opened and her moan became a cry as her body tightened from her neck to her calves. The cry stopped along with her breathing as it built and built and then she shattered.

Still in the throes of the rippling spasms, she wasn't sure how he was in front of her, standing, or how her arms had gotten around his neck. She was lifted then, her back pushed hard against the wall, her legs circling him and grabbing tight. Then he shoved himself into her, all the way, filling her, tearing another cry from her throat as her head hit the wall, as everything turned to white.

She came back to his kiss, to the taste of her sex, of his need. Grasping him by the back of his hair she kissed him ferociously, like an animal, as he pounded into her. As she rode his cock, breasts pressed tight against his chest, her heart pounding so hard he had to feel it.

Again and again, her back hit the wall, while she squeezed his hard, thick erection. There was nothing else, just the places her body met his, the places he was part of her.

He thrust once more, so hard she cried out, and he froze there, pinning her to the wall. She opened her eyes to watch him come, to see the way his orgasm ripped through his body.

She couldn't help it. She squeezed him as hard as she could the second his face relaxed. His gasp was louder than the jetting water, his thrust an involuntary response that made her feel powerful and wicked. She squeezed again, and after he jerked, he laughed.

"You're evil," he said, his voice all scratchy.

"Who, me?" she asked, batting her eyelashes, except her voice too was hoarse and uneven.

He kissed her again, then stepped back, easing her to the floor. "Yes, you. And as a reward, I'm going to wash every inch of your body with the greatest care. Trust me. You're going to like it."

She met his gaze, held him steady. "I do trust you."

He understood. She'd let him in, and the way he looked at her—humbled, honored—made her tremble.

Things had changed. Gone past the tipping point. There was no going back.

Oh, damn.

FEAR AND dread forced Dana to open her eyes. Something weighed on her belly. For a moment, she didn't recognize the teak-and-bamboo armoire. She turned her head toward the source of the light coming from the open bathroom door and saw Chase lying beside her, eyes closed. It was his arm that curled over her belly.

Not Bradford Morgan's. The consummate jerk.

Of all nights to have a dream about him.

She shoved the hair away from her face. The back of her neck was damp. Even though the dream seemed to have gone on forever, she knew dreams only lasted for a few seconds. That didn't help the clamminess of her skin or the depression soaking her with doubt. Was this thing with Chase a mistake? Was it her and Bradford all over again? But Chase wasn't married. He'd been honest with her, even about once having been engaged.

She looked at Chase again. No, this was totally different. She liked Chase, but had no illusions that their relationship would extend beyond the next few days. He couldn't boost her career, because she was done with show business.

Right?

Her throat seemed to tighten and she struggled for a breath. This was the dream talking. Taking her back to that horrid place. If she wanted anything from Chase, it was to give Kelly the break she deserved.

But he'd said nothing encouraging. In fact, he spoke so little of his business here. By now, didn't he at least trust her to reveal the playwright with whom he'd been meeting? Then again, why would he? She'd hardly been professional. The day after she swore she didn't date clients, she'd crawled into bed with him.

At the thought of her recklessness, a strangled gasp escaped her lips. His arm tightened around her, and, with eyes closed, he kissed the side of her shoulder. Staying very still, she looked past him at the digital clock on his side of the bed. One-thirty. Time to leave. Before she made matters worse by being seen on the guest floors or in the lobby.

Very slowly she lifted his arm away from her. He stirred a little, and she waited until she knew he was still deep in sleep before she moved away from him and set his arm down. She waited another few seconds before rolling out of bed. Her feet hit the carpet and she took her time shifting her weight off the mattress. He didn't budge so she quickly went into the bathroom and closed the door before gathering her clothes and getting dressed.

She had to get out of here before he awoke. He'd try to persuade her to stay, and she'd already demonstrated what a fool she was.

15

CHASE HAD been disappointed to find half his bed cold when he woke up, but he wasn't surprised. He knew she'd want to get out of the hotel before the morning shift change. But he wished she'd gotten him up or left a note. She had to have been really quiet because he was a light sleeper. Years of having to crash in hell holes undercover among thieves and dealers had taught him to sleep with one eye open and his hand not far from a weapon.

After he'd showered and dressed, he checked his cell phone for messages. He had five: one from Buddy, two from Roscoe, another from Gil, and a return call from yesterday, but nothing from Dana. He checked for missed calls and found that another person he'd tried contacting yesterday had called him back without leaving a message.

He automatically dismissed Roscoe's call. The guy was starting to be a real pain in the ass. Gil hadn't sounded urgent, but his ex-partner had. Besides, it was still early in Dallas so it had to be important. Could be Buddy had found some dirt on Kyle while doing the background check Chase had requested. That would make his day.

As soon as the call connected, Buddy said, "You get Susan's message? You need to get back here right away."

Chase frowned. He hadn't heard from the captain or his secretary. "Why?"

"IAD is getting ready to wrap things up."

"So? I've said everything that needs saying."

"It's Barker. He wants you to take a poly."

Chase muttered a pithy response. He hadn't done anything wrong, at least nothing every other UC officer had done at one time or another to maintain their cover. But that didn't mean you hadn't crossed the line now and then. It was that or find yourself looking down the wrong end of a Glock. Tough to get hooked up with the scumbags for the sake of your cover and come out squeaky clean. Barker knew that, the bastard. But he'd had it in for Chase ever since he'd beat Barker's son out of a promotion. A job that Barker thought Chase didn't deserve because of his tendency to occassionally break the rules.

"The review must be going my way if Barker is stooping that low."

"Possibly, man, but you don't wanna take no poly."

No, he didn't. There was always something that could go wrong with a polygraph. "When do they want me back?"

"Like yesterday. But I think they have the poly scheduled for tomorrow morning."

"Doesn't matter then. I doubt that I can be back in time."

There was a brief silence on the other end. "Barker is gunning for your badge. You're a good cop. Dedicated and ethical. I know that better than anyone. Don't give him an excuse to fire you."

Chase walked over to the window and stared at the gray clouds starting to blanket the city. Suited his mood perfectly. "I didn't get a message from the captain, or anyone else besides you." They both knew what that meant. Buddy swore colorfully, and Chase added, "They probably left a message on my machine at home."

"Chase, someone has it in for you. Honestly, I don't think it's the captain."

"No." But the man was weak. Too close to getting his pension. He wasn't about to shake things up in defense of Chase. He didn't blame the guy. They'd traveled a rocky road, him and the captain. Chase played it loose, and the captain liked to stick to the book. Somehow they hadn't gotten in each other's way too much. But Chase sure didn't expect the man to go to bat for him. He had a good idea who'd set him up, another cop he'd been forced to testify against last year, but he hadn't even voiced his suspicion to Buddy. Having an idea and hard evidence were two different things. No way would he accuse a fellow officer without proof.

"So what? Think you can get a plane back this afternoon?"

Chase scrubbed at his face. "Maybe, if I thought it would do any good."

"Come on, Culver, don't let the bastards win."

"Yeah." He sighed. "You find out anything on Kyle Williams?"

"The guy's a Boy Scout."

Not what he wanted to hear, but now he knew. "What about the two other names I gave you?"

"You're hangin' with a squeaky clean crowd these days. Sorry, man."

"Thanks." Good thing he wasn't expecting much. "Look, I gotta go. I have two leads to follow."

"Can I do anything else?"

"No."

"Can I talk you into getting on that freakin' plane?"

Chase smiled. "Nope." Then he disconnected the call and checked his watch. Mrs. Gillespie first, and then Gil. Except when he called Mrs. Gillespie back, she wasn't at her desk and he had to leave a message. Again.

Gil answered on the first ring, his voice gruff and harried, barking his name by way of a greeting. As soon as Chase identified himself, the head of security sighed heavily. "Just wanted to let you know we have another one."

"When?"

"Last night."

Before he could stop himself, Chase's cop's mind went straight to that place of suspicion. Didn't matter that he knew it couldn't be Dana. "You know what time?" he asked hesitantly.

"We're thinking between eleven and three. The guest whose room was hit had gone out to a club during that time."

That didn't mean anything. Dana had a good reason for wanting to sneak out in the middle of the night. Hiding in the bathroom while room service delivered dinner was easily explained, too. All of it was about maintaining her privacy. Perfectly reasonable. So why had the thought even crossed his mind? Last night she'd trusted him. She'd invited him to share an intimacy that had expressed that trust more than anything else could. He had to trust her, too.

He briefly closed his eyes. Hell, he could still taste her. "What did they take?"

"Made their best haul yet. Over fifty grand in jewelry. The couple was late meeting friends, the wife couldn't decide what to wear and by mistake ended up leaving the whole shebang on the bathroom counter. The thief was brazen, I'll tell you that. I doubled security two nights ago against normal hotel policy. I even added a camera near the elevators."

Brazen or confident. "Why is that against policy?"

"Guest privacy. We keep cameras in the back-of-the-house only."

"Ah, no." Gil muttered a foul curse. "My secretary just slipped me a note. Someone else just reported that they were robbed last night. I gotta go. The boys in blue are here now."

"One more thing…which floor got hit?"

Gil paused. "As a matter of fact, yours."

KELLY AND Amy were already sitting at a table, sipping glasses of chardonnay when Dana arrived at Annie's Diner. She was sticking to water. No more wine for her. At least not for the next decade or two. She didn't have a headache or anything, but she'd sure felt the effect, not the least of which was lowered inhibitions. She blushed just thinking about what he'd done to her last night, what she'd done to him.

The place was crowded, just like always. Although the decor was simple, in fact, totally lacking in imagination from its beige walls to its ancient, scarred, wooden tables, it was still their favorite place. The food was consistently yummy and priced right.

"Hey, kiddo." Amy moved a black patent-leather satchel with the signature leather-and-chain handles from the chair next to her to make room for Dana. "Glad you could make it."

"Why wouldn't I?" Dana frowned at the comment, but her gaze stayed on the awesome bag. "New purse?"

"I was feeling sorry for myself after work yesterday so I went shopping."

Dana settled in her seat and reached over to touch the gorgeous glossy leather. "Wow, this is a heck of a knockoff."

Amy and Kelly exchanged looks.

Dana's gaze went back to the Chanel logo. "It *is* a knockoff, isn't it?"

Amy sighed. "Let's say I'm going to be eating mac and cheese for the rest of the year."

Kelly shook her head. "You are crazy, girl."

Dana snorted. Amy was always complaining about money. "No kidding."

"I'd have gone with a Nancy Gonzalez myself," Kelly said flippantly, and she sipped her wine.

"Then you're both certifiable." Dana cast another longing glance at the bag. It truly was a beauty. Not that she'd fork out the couple of thousand it probably cost.

The waitress appeared to take Dana's iced tea order, and Kelly and Amy each asked for another chardonnay. The woman cleared two other empty glasses, and Dana realized her friends had had quite a headstart on her.

That was odd. Neither one drank much, especially not at noon. "Jeez, how long have you guys been here?"

"Not nearly long enough." Kelly raised her glass and then drained it.

"What is going on?" Her cell rang and she cringed, knowing who it was. She looked to be sure, just in case it was Chase. Not that she'd answer. She'd let him leave another message like he had earlier. But she saw who it was, which made the call so much easier to ignore.

When she put the phone back into her purse, Amy and Kelly gave her curious looks.

"It's Kyle," she said, rolling her eyes. "He's already left me two messages."

Amy frowned. "Did he say what it's about?"

"No, just that it's urgent. Yeah, right."

"You should probably talk to him," Amy said, and Kelly nodded her solemn agreement.

"Why in the world would I do that?"

"You haven't been to the hotel today?" Kelly asked glumly. Dana shook her head.

"There was another robbery," Amy said, equally sullen, and Kelly added, "Last night."

"How do you know?"

"Corrine called me right before I left my apartment," Amy said. "The police were there this morning, talking to employees. Maybe they're still there. I dunno."

"The police? I thought management was trying to keep this low-key."

Amy shrugged. "I doubt they can anymore. How many thefts have there been now? Five? Six?"

"At least." Dana thought about last night. She'd been there, at the St. Martine, sneaking out of Chase's suite probably at the same time a burglar was breaking into a room. Even worse, someone could have seen her leaving the hotel. She shivered. "But what does that have to do with Kyle calling me?"

Amy shrugged. "The police probably want to talk to you. Or maybe just security does. You haven't talked to them yet, have you?"

Dana swallowed. "No, but I really didn't think they'd consider me a suspect. I'm hardly ever there at night."

"I heard they're even talking to the guy that delivers the booze." Kelly frowned at her empty glass and then twisted around in her chair. "Where the hell is that waitress?"

"Calm down," Amy said irritably. "The place is packed. Cut her a break."

"How hard is it to pick up two glasses of wine from the bar, for God's sake?"

Amy met Dana's eyes and made a disgusted face. They never snapped at each other like that. The stress of the thefts was obviously getting to everyone. Including Dana. She quickly replayed her exit in the wee hours. The only person who possibly had seen her was the doorman, but she hadn't recognized him and anyway, he'd been talking to a kid delivering a bundle of newspapers.

"This whole thing sucks." Kelly gave up looking for the waitress and turned back to them. Her eyes were bloodshot, and she didn't look as if she needed anything else to drink, but Dana wasn't saying anything. "I'm glad I'm finally getting out of here. Should've left last week."

Amy looked as surprised as Dana. "You turned in your resignation?"

"Not yet. But I will as soon as we leave here."

Dana wished now more than ever that Chase had had some good news for her to pass on to Kelly. But if anything, Dana was more discouraged now than she had been in a long time. She reached across the table and touched her friend's hand. "Not today, okay? Wait until tomorrow."

"Why?"

"That's why," Amy said, glancing meaningfully at the glasses of wine the waitress set in front of them. "You don't look so hot."

"You wouldn't, either, if you got only three hours of sleep," Kelly said with an uncharacteristic belligerence before snatching her refill.

"You went clubbing without me?"

"You were too busy buying purses you can't afford."

Amy's gaze narrowed. "Excuse me?"

"Ready to order?" the waitress asked, unaware of the sudden tension.

Kelly held up her glass. "I'm fine."

"I'm not hungry," Amy muttered.

Dana smiled at the woman. "I think we need a few more minutes." The truth was, she wasn't hungry, either. This whole mess with Kelly leaving and the thefts was really getting to her. It didn't help that she was lacking in sleep, too.

As soon as the waitress left, Kelly said, "I was awful. I'm sorry."

Amy sighed. "Yeah, you are awful, but I still hate that you're leaving."

Kelly smirked. "Seriously, I wouldn't take that bag to work. You'd probably get hauled into security and given the third degree."

"That sucks, but you're probably right." Amy looked at Dana. "I wonder if they're questioning management, too. I heard Kyle paid a small fortune for those *Off the Mark* tickets the other night. Zoey in reservations said she heard he laid down a grand. He doesn't make that much money that he can afford to throw it around like that."

"I was wondering about his watch," Kelly said. "Looks like the real thing to me. A knockoff's second hand hesitates. A real Rolex's hand sweeps, and I tell you what, that puppy doesn't even hiccup."

"Wow." Amy's eyes widened. "That had to cost him over ten grand."

"Yep. I know he doesn't make enough to be wearing expensive stuff like that. No way."

Dana shook her head. "You know I don't like the guy, either, but let's not make assumptions. It isn't fair."

"Tell you what, Pollyanna," Kelly said, her mouth twisted wryly. "After you've been badgered by security, then talk to us."

"Come on." Amy made a sound of exasperation. "No need to get nasty."

"Who's getting nasty? I'm just keeping it real."

Dana stared at Kelly for a moment, the truth sinking in. She was worried. Security or the police had every reason to suspect her, especially if someone had seen her sneaking out of the hotel in the middle of the night. As much as she'd hate to admit why she'd been on the property, better to clear herself from their list of suspects. She dug into her purse for her wallet.

Kelly frowned at her. "What are you doing?"

She only had a couple of twenties and a ten, so she laid the ten on the table for her iced tea. "You're right. I'm going to see security."

Amy stared. "Right now?"

Kelly groaned. "Hey, I'm sorry. Don't pay any attention to me. I'm in a pissy mood."

Dana put her wallet back and slung her purse over her shoulder. "Might as well get it over with."

Her cell phone rang, and she glared at the screen. It was Kyle again. She let it ring long enough to switch over to voice mail, and then listened to the message. The police wanted to talk to her.

KYLE FLIPPED his cell phone closed, his palms clammy he was so steamed. Five messages. He'd left them over a period of four hours so he knew damn well she had to have gotten them. Stupid bitch. Even after dissing him, he was still trying to help her.

He noticed a stain on his desk from the bottom of his coffee mug and cursed a blue streak. No one would hear him. Not way back here in this small, windowless hellhole. His office was a joke. White walls, cheap prints and faded brown carpet. He was the only one who saw it, no guests ever came back here, but that wasn't the point.

When he'd lobbied for something bigger and better, the general manager had rebuffed him. Told him his place was at the front desk and mingling with the guests, not hiding out in his office. Yeah, but it was the old man shaking hands and having fancy dinners with the VIPs. Not Kyle. All he got were the complaints.

He stared at the morning report that he should've addressed by now, and then shoved it back into his in-box. The security report was the only thing he was interested in right now. Dana had been here last night. The security guard hadn't named her, but the description of a woman leaving the lobby at one this morning sure matched Dana. She'd been here because of Culver. She'd been banging that pompous prick. Kyle just knew it. Shit, the guy didn't even know how to dress.

Kyle adjusted his cuffs, pulled out the hand mirror he kept in his top drawer and checked the knot on his tie. Satisfied that every hair was in place, he returned the mirror to its spot near his breath spray and toothbrush, locked his desk and then, after he'd let himself out, locked his office door. He needed to start leaning harder on Gil, yet make sure the police weren't too visible. The guests didn't need to know what was going on. Although after last night, it might be difficult to keep matters quiet.

Gil had his door closed, but that didn't stop Kyle. He opened it and saw that Gil was on the phone. The older man gave him a warning look that he ignored. Screw him. Gil might report directly to the general manager, but in his absence, Kyle was technically the man's boss.

Gil cut the call short, hung up the phone and asked, "What do you want?"

Annoyed with his tone, Kyle allowed a silent moment to

pass, partly to check his composure and partly to let Gil stew. "Where are we on last night's theft?"

The oddest look flickered across Gil's face before it was replaced by the usual gruffness reserved for Kyle. "When I have something I'll let you know."

Kyle watched the man shuffle papers around, deliberately ignoring him, as if he weren't standing in his office. "I need to be kept in the loop."

Briefly looking up, Gil scowled. "Didn't I just tell you I'd let you know?"

Gil didn't like him. Kyle knew that, but the man was usually more smooth about it. Something was going on. "Are the police up in the guest's room?"

"Kyle—"

Gil's phone rang, and he paused long enough to give Kyle a menacing look before grabbing the receiver and barking his name. His expression and demeanor changed in a second.

"Mr. Roscoe, yes, of course," he said, and glanced nervously at Kyle.

Roscoe. The name rang a bell. A guest, he was pretty sure. Oh, yeah. He'd had a ring stolen.

Gil covered the mouthpiece and murmured, "I'll get back to you in the next twenty minutes." Grudgingly, he added, "You have my word."

Interesting. Obviously Gil really wanted to get rid of him. But what could he possibly have to say to a guest that was worth hiding from him? Kyle wasn't going to find the answer by sticking around.

"No problem," he said magnanimously, stepping back. "Talk to you later." He knew where to get Mr. Roscoe's phone number.

16

CHASE HAD just left the security office when he saw her enter the lobby. He had two phone calls to return, one from his captain and the other from IAD. But he didn't have time right now. Too much had happened too quickly in the past two hours. The conversation with Mrs. Gillespie had changed everything, taking him and Gil down another path. And now the police were involved with the lead. They were checking with the airlines and matching fingerprints. Chase was pretty sure he knew what they'd find, and Dana wouldn't be happy.

He really needed to talk to her. The police knew she'd been at the hotel last night because one of the security guards had seen her on camera get off the elevator. They hadn't positively ID'd her yet because the man didn't actually know who she was, but his camera shot was good enough even with her head down. Dana was too striking and not someone easy to overlook.

Knowing how much she valued her privacy, the decision hadn't been an easy one, but Chase admitted to Gil that Dana had been with him. The thing was, he couldn't account for all of her time. Hell, he didn't even know what time she'd left his room. Fortunately, it should be a moot point within a couple of hours.

Regardless of what the police discovered, he had to explain

who he was to Dana. He couldn't put off the inevitable any longer, even if it meant reimbursing Roscoe for every penny he'd paid Chase. Even if it meant that she hated him for the rest of her life—he just hoped she could find it in her heart to forgive him.

"Dana," he called out to her as she hurried past the front desk.

She glanced over, saw him, but didn't look as if she were inclined to stop.

"Wait up." He nearly knocked down a tourist trying to snap a picture of the lobby.

She didn't smile as he approached. Her arms were crossed, and he recognized the defensive posture. "I'm in kind of a hurry."

He wanted to touch her, to smooth the worried crease between her brows. With great effort, he kept his hands to himself. "I left you a couple of messages."

"I know."

He nodded. "I need to talk to you."

She looked tired, and her hair was coming loose from her ponytail. "It's going to have to wait." She gave him a wan smile. "Look, this isn't personal. I have some business to attend to."

"You're probably headed to security."

She blinked. "How do you know?"

"A lot's happened this morning."

"I heard." She hunched her shoulders, as if she were suddenly cold. "The police want to talk to me," she whispered. "They probably know I was here last night."

He took her by the arm and moved them farther away from the front desk, closer to the foyer in front of the ballrooms where there were no guests milling around. "Gil does. A security guard saw you."

Her face paled. "Great."

"I took the liberty of telling Gil you were with me."

A mixture of anger and fear flashed in her eyes. "You had no right."

"He's keeping the information to himself. I figured it was better he knew you had an alibi so he wouldn't give your name to the police."

She pursed her lips, resentment lingering on her face. "Then why do they want to talk to me?"

"You're not being singled out. You're on a list." He glanced around, and assured himself they couldn't be overheard. "We think we know who did it. I can't give you a name, but it should all be over by—"

"*We* think?" Her eyebrows dipped in a confused frown. "What do you mean by *we*?"

Chase exhaled sharply. This wasn't the place he wanted to do this. Admit that he'd been lying through his teeth. He'd been good at undercover work because he was an ace at manipulation, he could bullshit a bullshitter without breaking a sweat.

Ironically, he'd been the one doing all the acting for the past week. While on the job he'd plied his trade hundreds of times without blinking. Except the situation had always revolved around the scum of the earth and he hadn't given the lies a second thought. But this time Dana had been his victim and there was no way to sugarcoat it.

He had to tell her the truth, but even without all the deception, would she want him then? Women like her got any man they wanted. Not a loser like him. His job had been the only thing to be proud of and he'd blown that.

She waited expectantly, the innocence in her beautiful blue eyes making him feel lower than a rattlesnake.

He cleared his throat. "Maybe this isn't the time to—"

"Good afternoon, Mr. Culver." Kyle walked up, directing his oily smile at Chase. "Or is it Cutter?"

Chase's heart sank to the toes of his pointed black boots. It took all his restraint not to shove his fist in the guy's smug face. How had he found out? Gil? No, Gil didn't even know his real name.

Dana looked from him to Kyle and then back to Chase again. "What's going on?"

"You don't want to do this, Williams," Chase told him in a low warning voice.

"Do what?" he asked, all phony innocence, except for the shrewdness in his eyes. "Am I mistaken? It is Cutter, isn't it?"

Although he kept his murderous gaze on Kyle, Chase felt the weight of Dana's stare boring into him. His fault. His reaction had to make her curious as hell. "You wanna take the chance of blowing up this investigation?" Chase asked calmly.

The guy's smile faltered. He hesitated, glanced at Dana, and apparently found his balls again. "I just got off the phone with Leroy Roscoe. You know, the guy who hired you, Cutter. He's very anxious to get his ring back. He'd like to know if you've made any progress."

Staring at the shorter man, Chase clenched his hands into fists as he fought for control. He couldn't even look at Dana. The truth was bad enough, but to have it come from Kyle…

"Chase, please, tell me what's going on." Dana's voice broke, and she stepped back, her arms wrapped around herself.

"My apologies." Kyle's eyes glinted with malice. "I probably shouldn't have said anything in front of Dana. After all, I imagine she's a suspect."

Chase stepped forward for Kyle, but Dana stopped him.

"Don't," she said, getting in between them. "Whatever it is, it's not worth it."

"You might be wrong about that," Kyle said, snorting, and taking a step back. "Tell her, Officer Cutter."

Dana froze. Her back was to Kyle so she didn't see the satisfied smirk on his arrogant face. Not that it mattered one bit. The anger and disappointment and disbelief in her glassy eyes were all because of Chase. Kyle had only been the messenger.

"Chase?" she said slowly, looking at him, confusion and panic mounting in her face. Her lips parted and, shaking her head, she started to back away, the whole thing happening in slow motion.

"Dana, wait. Let me explain."

Kyle scoffed. "Let's hear it, Officer Cutter."

Chase ignored him.

A disturbance erupted in the lobby. Gil walked briskly past them, throwing them a brief glance, but his attention was clearly focused on what was going on near the front desk.

Chase turned back to Dana, but she'd bolted. He twisted around in time to see her run past the two uniformed police officers and the portly doorman holding open the front door.

CHASE COULDN'T remember being more scared and angry in his entire life. Kelly and Amy had walked in and were met by the police officers. Obviously the prints had come back and his call to Gillespie, the bank manager, had paid off. Gil waved him over, and as much as Chase wanted to run after Dana, he knew this was something he had to take care of first.

He glared at Kyle. "You and me, we're not finished," he said as he walked away.

"But you and Dana are."

Tempted to punch the victorious grin off the guy's face, Chase kept going. Straight toward Gil and the officer talking to a frightened-looking Kelly. Not too many guests were in the lobby at this time of day, but the few who were milling about were glued to the commotion.

"Let's take this to my office," Gil was saying to the officers. His gaze went to Kelly, and Chase noticed her pale face, eyes red, lower lip quivering. "Follow me," Gil instructed.

"This wasn't supposed to happen," she murmured. "I didn't plan any of this. It was Eduardo. He was— Oh my God." She swiped at the tears sliding down her cheeks. "It was all just talk. A fantasy. You have to believe me."

"We'll discuss this in private," Gil said in a low, stern voice.

"I'm so ashamed."

Gil gently touched her arm. "Ms. Wilson, please, we want to hear your side. But I doubt you want to do it out here."

Kelly scanned the faces of the people who'd gathered around them, almost as if she'd just realized where she was. She looked as if she might turn and run, so Chase stepped in behind her. Her defeated eyes briefly met his and then she nodded and meekly followed Gil and one of the officers, while the other uniform walked alongside her. Chase brought up the rear, putting up a restraining hand when Amy tried to follow them.

"What's going on?" she asked, but the fearful expression on her disbelieving face indicated she had the right idea.

"Someone will come out and explain everything," Chase said, and then pausing, added, "You probably ought to stick around. Kelly might need you."

Resentment and accusation darkened her eyes. "Who are you?"

He ignored her and kept walking. Dana was the only one he owed an explanation to. Her forgiveness was what he wanted. He doubted he'd get it.

CHASE GOT out of the cab and checked the address Gil had given him. The neighborhood was okay, seemed safe enough, but what a sorry-looking redbrick apartment building. Even the dump he rented back in Dallas was better than this place with the peeling windowsills and dented front door.

"Should I wait?" the cabbie asked, and Chase shook his head and closed the car door.

Probably being overly optimistic. Dana either wouldn't let him in or she'd slam the door in his face. But Chase had to try. He couldn't leave the city without explaining. Without laying out how he felt about her. He sure was nervous.

He slowly climbed the steps, netting a curious look from one of Dana's neighbors smoking on the stoop. He went through the open doorway and noticed an elevator at the far end of the narrow foyer past the two rows of built-in metal mailboxes, but decided on the stairs.

"Can I help you?" the woman asked, following close behind.

"I'm looking for Dana McGuire," he said, even though he knew her apartment number. "Third floor, right?"

"That's right, but she isn't home."

"You sure?"

"Left about ten minutes ago," she said, putting one hand on her ample hip and sizing him up. "Dressed in her running clothes."

"Shit." He winced at his bad manners, and pushed a weary hand through his hair. "Sorry."

The woman's face creased in a thoughtful frown, and then, as if deciding a serial killer wouldn't be wearing a dress shirt, slacks and a tie, she said, "I think her roommate is up there. She might know when Dana's coming back."

"Thanks." He couldn't wait. He needed to talk to Dana now, and he figured he knew where she was. Worth a shot, anyway. Damn, he wished he'd hung on to that cab.

He waved his thanks to the woman and didn't stop until he got to the corner, where he hoped to spot a taxi. None were in sight, but he knew if he waited for a few minutes one was bound to show up. Turned out she lived only some thirty-odd blocks from Central Park, a distance she probably jogged in fifteen or twenty minutes, but it was hot and humid and he was wearing cowboy boots.

It didn't take long for a cab to drop off a fare, and Chase caught the driver as he pulled away from the curb. Late-afternoon traffic had picked up and the ride to the park seemed to take forever. They finally got there, and Chase hopped out right in the middle of the park since he had no exact idea where she'd be. He knew the route she'd taken him and he figured that if he didn't stray too far she'd pass him at some point. With his luck she'd probably chosen to run along the Hudson, but he was betting she was here somewhere.

After about fifteen minutes of briskly walking the path, feeling pretty foolish, he sank onto a nearby bench and loosened his tie. The sun was hotter than blazes and he was tired from having too little sleep in the past five days. Why had he thought he could find her in a park this big? He was losing it. That he cared less about what was happening with IAD back in Dallas was proof alone. His career was on the line and he'd been so wrapped up with Dana and making sure he proved her innocent that he hadn't even made so much as a phone call.

Though he was still pretty angry at the department and i▸
they were on a witch hunt it didn't matter if he cooperated o▸
not. Besides, he was suspended without pay, so screw them
He wasn't working on their nickel. If he was out of town, they
could just wait until he got back. And if that meant they fired
him, well he'd worry about that if the time came. Right now
Dana was his main concern.

He checked his watch and considered going back to the
corner deli he'd noticed near her apartment. From the place
he'd be able to see her approach from either direction. No, he
couldn't wait. He'd take a complete lap around first…

Chase saw her then, coming around the bend where a group
of kids kicked a soccer ball around in the grass. She was still
far away, but he'd recognize her lean grace from twice the
distance. Naturally, she wouldn't want to see him, and once
she spotted him, he hoped she didn't turn and run the other
way. He stayed on the bench, trying to keep a low profile,
waiting for her to get closer.

She apparently didn't see him until he stood. And then she
slowed down. He didn't need to see her face to know she was
thinking about taking off in the other direction. He started
toward her, and she stopped and waited, which was more than
he expected.

He had the disadvantage of the sun shining directly into his
face, making it difficult to gauge her expression. He shaded
his eyes, and when he saw the pain in hers, he lowered his
hand. "Dana, we need to talk."

"We have nothing to say to each other."

"I'm so sorry you found out like that."

"You're sorry I found out, period."

"No, I was going to tell you. Today."

"Right."

"It's the truth. I wanted to tell you earlier, but I had an obligation to my client."

She hesitated, curiosity in her voice when she said, "I thought you were a cop."

"I am. But not right now. I was working as a private detective. Long story."

"But you're so good at telling stories."

He smiled wryly at her sarcasm. Anything she could fling, he deserved. "Can we go somewhere cooler to talk?"

Without warning, she started running again. Not jogging. Running. And not toward someplace cooler, he suspected.

If two women talking and pushing strollers hadn't taken up the path, blocking her way, he would never have caught up with her. "Come on, Dana. Give me a chance."

"Get lost."

"I'm in street clothes. This isn't fair."

She slowed down long enough to glare at him. A sheen of moisture coated her face and escaped tendrils of hair clung to her cheeks and neck. "Don't you dare talk to me about what's fair."

He threw up his hands in supplication. "You're right. I apologize."

"I don't want your apology," she muttered through clenched teeth. "I want you to go away."

"I will. I promise. Just hear me out first."

Her response was to pick up speed again, leaving him behind.

Already out of breath, he gave it all he had, and charged after her. "I'm not giving up even if I have to follow you home and sit outside all night."

She ignored him, staying several yards ahead of him.

"Goddamn it, Dana, all I want to do is explain, and then you never have to see me again."

Children playing on the path slowed her down again, but it was no use. He couldn't keep up, not wearing boots and with his side hurting like a son of a bitch. He'd do just like he said and wait at her apartment. Probably better to let her calm down, anyway. At this point he didn't have a choice.

He stopped and bent over, crippled by the sudden shooting pain attacking the area below his ribs. Great, this was just great.

17

DANA NEEDED water. She'd been running too long without hydrating, but she refused to stop. Not until he left the park. Better yet, went back to Texas or wherever he was really from.

He was a cop. And a liar, a thief in his own right. He'd stolen her trust, her sanity. She'd finally made peace with her life, found a satisfying career, but he'd inspired hope again. She hadn't wanted the seed to sprout, and she hadn't actually realized how quickly the hope had flourished until the dream was again ripped away. He'd used her, and sadly, she'd embraced his deception. Far, far worse, disillusion with the man himself cut her to the quick.

As angry as she was with him, she was twice as upset with herself. Humiliated. Horrified. How could she have been so naive? So absurdly foolish? The signs that he was an imposter had all been there. The rough edge, the scars, a gunshot wound, for heaven's sake. But she'd blithely chosen to ignore common sense. She'd behaved like a total idiot. How could she ever look at herself in the mirror again?

Tears welled, threatening to further her humiliation, and in case any had spilled, she used the back of her forearm to wipe her face. Salty perspiration burned her eyes and she muttered a curse.

No one heard. Silence had followed her for the past couple

of minutes, and, in spite of herself, she slowed down and
glanced over her shoulder. Chase had disappeared. Had he
given up and returned to the hotel or had he gone to her apartment as he'd threatened? No, he didn't know where she lived.
Although he'd probably run a background check on her.

The sudden thought made her mad all over again, but she
was so tired she didn't know how much farther she could run.
She wanted to go home, take a warm bath, eat two pints of
cookie dough ice cream and then cry herself to sleep. If he
showed up, she'd call the police, tell them he was stalking her.
He was one of them. They'd let him go, but she'd at least have
the satisfaction of totally ruining his night.

He'd hurt her. Badly. The only thing worse would be
allowing him to see how much. And then there was Kelly.
Good-natured, hopeful, talented Kelly. She wasn't a
criminal. She was just—how could she have stooped to such
a horrible thing? Why hadn't Dana seen how troubled her
friend had become? Maybe it was all a mistake. She prayed
that it was.

Annoyingly disoriented, she looked around for the best way
out of the park. The ducks gliding on the lake should've told
her where she was, but her brain was a scrambled mess. She
spun around and then she saw Chase. Doubled over, just off the
path, in the grassy area where people often picnicked. With a
ball in his hands, a young boy stood staring at him. The child's
mouth moved, he was saying something to Chase, who didn't
respond.

Oh God, was it his wound? Had he hurt himself trying to
keep up with her? What did she care? His problem. He had a
cell phone. He could dial 911. Excellent logic, except she
couldn't stop herself. Her heart pounding from more than
exertion, she jogged toward him, anxious because he hadn't

even looked up. Still hunched over, he took off his tie, and then planted both palms on his thighs.

"Chase?"

Without straightening, he turned his flushed face toward her. "What's wrong? Is it your wound?"

"He was groaning," the boy supplied.

"I'm okay, kid," Chase said, his voice ragged. "Your mom's calling you. Go."

The boy turned toward the woman standing near the lake, her hands cupped around her mouth as she hollered for the child. He waved acknowledgment and then looked solemnly at Dana as he backed away. "You take over, okay?"

She nodded, her gaze going back to Chase. "Tell me right now, are you hurt?"

He hesitated, and then slowly straightened. "Just out of breath."

"Jerk." Before she could get away, he grabbed her wrist. "Let me go, or I swear I'll deck you."

A weary smile curved his mouth.

"This was low, really low." She twisted her hand but his grip was too strong.

"I wasn't trying to trick you," he said, his voice uneven, his eyes searching hers. "I feel as if my friggin' heart is gonna explode."

Hers already had. Into a million pieces. "You'll survive."

He snorted, his expression thoughtful and faraway. "Maybe not this time." He stroked the underside of her wrist with the pad of his thumb. His cell phone rang, and she thought this might be her chance to get away, but he ignored it. "The thing is, I'm not going anywhere until we talk. If it's not here, then at your apartment, even if I have to camp outside."

"You don't know where I live."

His confident expression told her otherwise. Fresh anger erupted in the pit of her stomach. Nausea alone kept her rooted to the spot.

Chase sighed. "If you want to get rid of me, let me explain."

"You don't let me go, I'll scream. A cop will be here in seconds."

"I'll flash my badge."

"Go to hell."

"Dana, I know you're angry and confused right now. You have every right, but we need to talk. You're gonna need closure, and after today I won't be here to answer your questions."

"Promise?"

He loosened his hold. "Promise."

The thought of never seeing him again didn't appease her in a way one might expect, which only served to make her angry all over again. She pulled her hand away and resentfully rubbed the skin he'd touched. As much as she hated to admit it, he had a point. She knew herself. She'd always wonder what had happened, why he'd chosen to con her. She'd replay the last week over and over in her mind until she made herself crazy.

He must've taken her lengthened silence for weakness because he suggested, "Why don't we go find some shade?"

Her gaze automatically went to a bench under the massive branches of an old pin oak. Not that she'd decided to give in. But he did look a bit pale now that the flush was subsiding. Big deal. His fault.

"Dana?"

"I'm thinking," she snapped, knowing she was going to give in, not knowing if she would hate herself for it.

He threw up his hands. "Okay."

She pulled the elastic band from her hair and then redid her ponytail. Without saying a word, she walked toward the bench, not bothering to see if he followed. She sank onto the scarred wood, and then stared at a couple playing with an orange Frisbee. She wasn't sure why she was still here. He couldn't say anything that would change her mind. He was a sneaky bastard, and she was a stupid sucker, and that was that.

He sat on the opposite end and rolled back his shirt sleeves to the middle of his forearm. "This is crazy, but I'm not sure where to begin."

"Who are you?"

"Well, you know now I'm a cop." He half laughed. "That is, I hope I'm still a cop. I work for the Dallas police department as an undercover operative."

She still didn't believe him. "And they sent you halfway across the country for this."

"This is private work I've been doing." He noisily cleared his throat. "I'm on suspension with the department."

She squinted at him, saw his jaw tighten, not sure if she wanted to ask the obvious question. Instead, she asked, "Who's Roscoe?"

"He was a guest here last month. He hired me to get back a ring that was stolen."

"So you decided to pretend you were a big-shot producer who was going to be hiring?"

"No, not until I met you." His eyes reluctantly met hers. "I figured that was the best way to get to you."

The air seemed to flee her lungs. "You thought I was the thief?"

"You were on the short list."

"That's why the dinners, the—" Her voice caught. She would've gotten up if she'd thought her legs would hold her.

"No." He moved closer. "No. I knew you weren't the perp the first day we met."

"You're a liar."

"I can be. It's my job. I'm good at it." He stared deep into her eyes, his filled with regret. Not that it mattered. "I didn't think twice about telling you what I thought you wanted to hear. Am I sorry? I can't begin to tell you how much."

"Gee, that changes everything."

His elbows braced on his thighs, his hands clasped, he hung his head and stared at his hands. "I've been doing under-cover work for nine years. I work with some really bad people. If I can't fool them, I'm dead."

She laughed humorlessly. "Yeah, I was such a threat."

"I'm just saying," he murmured. "That's what I do, it's not who I am."

She wrapped her arms around herself and shivered despite the warm humid air. "I don't know who you are."

"You do." He abruptly swung toward her. "I didn't lie about myself, only my profession. The part about my parents, my dropping out of college, the small-town upbringing, all of that is true."

"Only because it was easier to keep your story straight."

"That's true, too. But I also let my guard down with you. I told you things I never talk about."

Grudgingly, the admission pleased her, but of course he could be lying. After all, he worked undercover, that's what he did. "How did you know I wasn't the thief?"

"My gut. Although I admit, it wasn't easy eliminating you as a suspect."

"That's crazy. I'm never at the hotel at night when the thefts occurred." The words were barely out of her mouth when she recognized their absurdity. She'd broken her own rule by seeing him in his suite. Not once, but twice.

He didn't say anything, nor did he have to.

She looked down at her sneakers. "Tell me about Kelly."

"She's in custody."

"I figured that much."

"She had an accomplice. The guy she'd been seeing. We think he's someone wanted by Interpol. He's the person the police want, not Kelly. If she cooperates, they'll go easy on her."

Dana's heart sank. Had she been that bad a friend? She hadn't even sensed Kelly was in trouble. No, this wasn't real. None of it. "It's a mistake. Kelly wouldn't do this. She was going back home. She has a job waiting…"

Chase shook his head. "There's no job. It was just a story she told everyone to explain why she was about to suddenly leave town."

"No, her mother wrote her letters…"

"There were no letters."

"You don't know that—"

"Dana, there are only two banks in Kelly's hometown. I called them both and spoke to the managers. Neither had heard of Kelly."

"You called?"

He nodded slowly, his reluctance tipping her off to the part she'd played.

"I told you about Kelly," she whispered, her stomach clenching painfully again. "You used me to get information on my friends."

"Besides the fact that it was my job, I would have used anything I could get to clear your name. I won't apologize. I'd do it all over again."

"Don't give me that load of crap. I couldn't have been a serious suspect."

"The list was getting shorter and you were on it."

"That doesn't make sense," she said, yet in a way she knew

All or Nothing

he was probably right. "Anyway, I don't care. Kelly is my friend."

"So she should get a pass?" The hard glint in his eyes made him look like a cop. "She's a thief. She broke the law."

Dana understood, but still, she didn't want to hear it. "You gave her hope, you know. She thought you were seriously looking for talent. I hate you for that."

He stared at her for a long uncomfortable moment and then asked, "Was it Kelly who had the hope, or you?"

Outraged, she couldn't believe he'd just said that. "I told you—" She cut herself short, her voice suddenly untrustworthy.

"I know what you told me," he said quietly. "And I jumped right on it. Convinced myself that I was absolved because you wouldn't care when you found out that I wasn't going to be able to boost your career. But I knew…deep down I knew you still wanted that big break…" He looked away. "For that I can't forgive myself."

"You have a lot of nerve. You don't know me." Damn it, he was right. She'd started to hope. She'd even mentally planned the phone call she'd make to her parents.

His cell phone rang again, and annoyance flashed across his face. He yanked it out of his pocket, but instead of answering it, he switched it to vibrate.

She should go. He'd had his say, and she'd heard just about everything she wanted to hear. Except for one thing. "Why were you suspended?"

His mouth curved in a wry smile. "I screwed up an undercover job I'd been working on for almost a year. A lot of time and department resources went down the tubes." He straightened and gripped the bench on either side of his thighs, his knuckles turning white. "The worst of it, a woman was killed.

And a very evil man who should've been put away is still selling heroin to schoolkids."

Sympathy managed to slink past her resolve. "Is that when you got shot?"

He nodded, his face straight ahead, his gaze on something in the distance. "Should've been me lying on a slab in the morgue and not Carmen Rios."

The thought chilled Dana to the bone. "You didn't shoot her." She paused. "Did you?"

"No." He looked at her then, the devastation in his eyes hard to witness. "But I didn't protect her, either."

She swallowed. "Tell me about it."

Clearly, he didn't want to, but he took a deep breath and said, "I've worked undercover my entire career. They plucked me right out of the academy before I picked up telltale habits. Even while he's wearing plain clothes, you can spot a cop a mile away, the way he stands, the way he drives…" One side of his mouth went up. "The shiny shoes. That's why the department likes to grab candidates before they put on the uniform."

"I dated a cop once." She hadn't thought about Mark in forever, a homicide detective she'd met when she first arrived in New York. "I went to dinner with him a couple of times and he had to sit with his back to the wall."

"Exactly what I'm talking about." He gave her a crooked smile. "I see you like cops."

Sorry she'd sidestepped the conversation or had given him the impression that everything was okay between them, she didn't return the smile. "What happened to ruin your operation or whatever you call it?"

"I was in deep cover. Miguel Sanchez was our target. It took me almost a year of living around his filth to get close to him. We were days away from nailing him and all of a sudden my boss calls a raid. They found out Miguel knew I was a cop so they had to get me out."

"If there was a raid, then you got him."

"You don't understand. We had nothing—" He cringed suddenly and put a hand to his heart.

Anxious, she leaned toward him, but it was only the phone vibrating in his breast pocket. "Answer it, darn it. Maybe it's about Kelly."

He glanced at the screen. "It's not."

"Someone is trying awfully hard to get a hold of you."

"It's just my ex-partner." He started to turn off the phone and then muttered a curse, and as he stood, said, "I'm sorry. Wait. Please."

She stayed where she was and watched him walk a few feet away before answering the call. He kept his agitated voice low, but she picked up enough to know that he was talking about returning to Dallas. Tonight, if she heard correctly. Good. The sooner he was out of her life the better. Yeah, right. As if he'd been in her life to begin with. She'd merely been a means to an end.

This time he did turn off the phone as he reclaimed his side of the bench. "No more interruptions."

"What time is your flight?"

"I haven't booked one yet."

"I couldn't help overhearing. It sounded as if you need to go back right away."

He shrugged uncomfortably. "The department wants me there so they can wrap up my review tomorrow morning."

"And take you off suspension?"

"That, or fire me."

Dana hesitated. She did not want to get involved with this

man. There was nothing more to say. "I still don't understand what you did wrong."

"The God's honest truth is, I don't, either." Staring off into the distance, his face creased in an anguished frown. "They said I blew my own cover, that I leaked information. I went over the last few months in my head a hundred times and I don't see it." He slid her a reluctant look. "I'm not the most popular guy in the department. I kind of have a reputation as a loose cannon. Few people would hate to see me go."

She thought for a moment. "So you think someone might have framed you?"

"It crossed my mind."

She stared at him, curiosity gnawing at her. The possibility had done more than cross his mind. "Why are you here wasting time instead of back in Dallas fighting for your job?"

"I had business here," he said quietly.

"Well, you've caught the big, bad thief, so now you're free to go."

His sad smile stirred sympathy she didn't want to feel. "Yep, I'm free to go."

She blinked when she realized he was about to stand. In spite of herself, she didn't want him to leave. Could she have been so wrong about him? Were her instincts that poor? No, she didn't believe that. As soon as he'd solved the case he could've been in a cab to the airport. But he'd come after her. "Why did you stay?"

"You have to ask?"

"Tell me," she whispered around the lump in her throat.

"I wanted to make sure you were okay. I wanted you to hear the truth from me. Not Gil. Not Kyle." He smiled. "You know how the hotel grapevine can be."

She thought about how she'd hidden in the bathroom when

room service had delivered their dinner. How she'd told him she never dated clients. "I gave you so many reasons to suspect me."

"You did keep me on my toes." He frowned suddenly. "How do you know Leroy Roscoe?"

"I don't."

"He specifically asked me to check you out."

She shook her head. "I don't recall the name—wait a minute. Is he tall with white hair and bushy eyebrows and had a heavy southern accent?"

"That's him. Bet he hit on you."

"Sure did."

"Sorry about that. He's not really a friend. More like an acquaintance I made during my misspent youth."

Dana met his eyes, a sudden and unpleasant thought dawning. "Everything you told me about your childhood, was it true?"

"Every bit of it."

"So all those people back home had to eat their words when you became a cop."

He smiled wryly. "See, that's what you call irony because even working light undercover, it's better you play the role of badass all the time."

"So they won't know unless you get fired." How was that for irony?

He briefly lost the smile. But then he shrugged, like it didn't matter. Except she knew better. It did matter. If he was fired and disgraced, it would hurt. A lot.

"You've got to book a flight. Now."

"What?"

"Come on, call the airlines. Don't let them get away with this."

"Wait. Dana." He reached for her arm. "About us—does this mean—?"

"I don't know. Okay. I don't." She breathed in deeply. Maybe she was still being a fool, but in spite of everything, she felt as if she knew this man, and she didn't want to see him hurt. "Right now I want you to go fight for your job. Later, we'll see about us."

He lifted her chin and looked deeply into her eyes. "I came here to do a job. You were unexpected. I never meant to hurt you."

"I know."

"I'm coming back."

She leaned into him, whispering, "This is for luck." And then she kissed him.

Epilogue

One year later, Outside Dallas, Texas

"Ms. McGuire, why don't you have your own kids?" Sweet, blond, eight-year-old Sally Ann Hawkins stared up at Dana with her pretty, wide, blue eyes. "My mama says that before you know it, you're gonna be too old and you'll be real sorry."

Dana heard laughing, and looked up to see Chase leaning against the door frame of her dance studio.

"Yeah, Ms. McGuire, I gotta say, you are getting rather long in the tooth." He winked at Dana, who gave him a wry look, and then he walked in and tugged at one of the girl's pigtails. "Well, Miss Sally Ann, I do believe you're getting prettier every time I see you."

The little girl's pointy chin went up, a grin splitting her freckled face. "Mama says I'm gonna win the Sade County Junior Miss contest this year."

"You know, I believe your mama is right." He inclined his head toward the door. "She's outside in the car waiting for you."

"Thanks, Officer Chase." She flashed him a smile, her rosy cheeks dimpling, and then grabbed her backpack. "See you on Wednesday, Ms. McGuire," she called over her shoulder as she scampered out of the building.

Sighing, Dana stared at the doorway, grateful Sally was

the last one. The other nine girls in her dance class had left a few minutes ago. She was tired today, and Sally Ann's comment about winning the County Junior Miss pageant had struck a sour note.

Chase closed the distance between them, wrapped his arms around her, lifted her in the air and kissed her soundly.

"Hey." She pushed at his arm. "One of the kids might duck back in."

He put her back down. "So? They apparently know you're old enough to be making out."

"Very funny." She grabbed a towel she'd hung on the ballet bar and snapped it at him.

Chuckling, he jumped back. "Watch the family jewels, darlin', especially with you not getting any younger."

She rolled her eyes and draped the towel around her damp neck. She really hadn't worked all that hard, but she was exhausted.

He squinted at her. "What's wrong?"

Dana used the towel to blot the side of her neck and cheek. "Just tired, that's all." A weak smile tugged at the corners of her mouth.

"How about your parents, have they made their plane reservations for Thanksgiving yet?"

She groaned. "They are so nervous. I told Daddy we could go there instead now that you're a nine-to-fiver, but he insists that they need to broaden their horizons."

"Nine-to-fiver," he repeated. "Makes me sound old and boring."

"Excuse me. This from the man who accused me of being long in the tooth." She slid her arms around his waist, and his arms immediately came around her. "Are you ever sorry you aren't working undercover anymore?"

"Nope. I like training all those raw recruits. Besides, it's nice not to get shot at anymore."

She shuddered. After IAD had cleared him he'd gone back to light undercover work. Waiting for his phone call each night had been nerve-racking. When the opening for an academy instructor came up, he'd surprised the entire department by applying for the position. She knew he'd done it for her, and she loved him for giving her that peace of mind.

"I still can't believe your parents are willing to fly here," he said. "When we were there last month your dad asked me how long I thought it would take for them to drive."

Dana shrugged. "Knowing them, they're probably figuring that if grandkids came along they'd better be able to visit often."

"Grandkids?" Chase laughed unevenly.

Her belly fluttered and her hand automatically went there. He stared at her. "Are you trying to tell me something?"

"No, no, no." She quickly lowered her hand. "I've just been feeling a little off today."

Disappointment flickered in his face. "Hope you're not coming down with something."

"Me, too." She nibbled at her lip. "What would happen if I did…you know?"

A wide smile curved his mouth and he pulled her close. "I'd be the happiest guy west of the Mississippi."

Dana pressed her cheek against his chest and sighed with contentment. Her hand went to her tummy. Maybe she was pregnant and didn't know it. She closed her eyes and smiled. She wouldn't mind that at all.

* * * * *

Turn the page for a sneak preview of
AFTERSHOCK, *a new anthology*
featuring New York Times *bestselling author*
Sharon Sala.

Available October 2008.

n●cturne™

Dramatic and sensual tales of paranormal romance.

Chapter 1

October
New York City

Nicole Masters was sitting cross-legged on her sofa while a cold autumn rain peppered the windows of her fourth-floor apartment. She was poking at the ice cream in her bowl and trying not to be in a mood.

Six weeks ago, a simple trip to her neighborhood pharmacy had turned into a nightmare. She'd walked into the middle of a robbery. She never even saw the man who shot her in the head and left her for dead. She'd survived, but some of her senses had not. She was dealing with short-term memory loss and a tendency to stagger. Even though she'd been told the problems were most likely temporary, she waged a daily battle with depression.

Her parents had been killed in a car wreck when she was

twenty-one. And except for a few friends—and most recently her boyfriend, Dominic Tucci, who lived in the apartment right above hers, she was alone. Her doctor kept reminding her that she should be grateful to be alive, and on one level she knew he was right. But he wasn't living in her shoes.

If she'd been anywhere else but at that pharmacy when the robbery happened, she wouldn't have died twice on the way to the hospital. Instead of being grateful that she'd survived, she couldn't stop thinking of what she'd lost.

But that wasn't the end of her troubles. On top of everything else, something strange was happening inside her head. She'd begun to hear odd things: sounds, not voices—at least, she didn't think it was voices. It was more like the distant noise of rapids—a rush of wind and water inside her head that, when it came, blocked out everything around her. It didn't happen often, but when it did, it was frightening, and it was driving her crazy.

The blank moments, which is what she called them, even had a rhythm. First there came that sound, then a cold sweat, then panic with no reason. Part of her feared it was the beginning of an emotional breakdown. And part of her feared it wasn't—that it was going to turn out to be a permanent souvenir of her resurrection.

Frustrated with herself and the situation as it stood, she upped the sound on the TV remote. But instead of *Wheel of Fortune,* an announcer broke in with a special bulletin.

"This just in. Police are on the scene of a kidnapping that occurred only hours ago at The Dakota. Molly Dane, the six-year-old daughter of one of Hollywood's block-buster stars, Lyla Dane, was taken by force from the family apartment. At this time they have yet to receive a ransom demand. The housekeeper was seriously injured during the abduction, and is, at the present time, in surgery. Police are hoping to be able to talk to her once she regains consciousness. In the meantime, we are going now to a press conference with Lyla Dane."

Horrified, Nicole stilled as the cameras went live to where the actress was speaking before a bank of microphones. The shock and terror in Lyla Dane's voice were physically painful to watch. But even though Nicole kept upping the volume, the sound continued to fade.

Just when she was beginning to think something was wrong with her set, the broadcast suddenly switched from the Dane press conference to what appeared to be footage of the kidnapping, beginning with footage from inside the apartment.

When the front door suddenly flew back against the wall and four men rushed in, Nicole gasped. Horrified, she quickly realized that this must have been caught on a security camera inside the Dane apartment.

As Nicole continued to watch, a small Asian woman, who she guessed was the maid, rushed forward in an effort to keep them out. When one of the men hit her in the face with his gun, Nicole moaned. The violence was too reminiscent of what she'd lived through. Sick to her stomach, she fisted her hands against her belly, wishing it was over, but unable to tear her gaze away.

When the maid dropped to the carpet, the same man followed with a vicious kick to the little woman's midsection that lifted her off the floor.

"Oh my God," Nicole said. When blood began to pool beneath the maid's head, she started to cry.

As the tape played on, the four men split up in different

directions. The camera caught one running down a long marble hallway, then disappearing into a room. Moments later he reappeared, carrying a little girl, who Nicole assumed was Molly Dane. The child was wearing a pair of red pants and a white turtleneck sweater, and her hair was partially blocking her abductor's face as he carried her down the hall. She was kicking and screaming in his arms, and when he slapped her, it elicited an agonized scream that brought the other three running. Nicole watched in horror as one of them ran up and put his hand over Molly's face. Seconds later, she went limp.

One moment they were in the foyer, then they were gone.

Nicole jumped to her feet, then staggered drunkenly. The bowl of ice cream she'd absentmindedly placed in her lap shattered at her feet, splattering glass and melting ice cream everywhere.

The picture on the screen abruptly switched from the kidnapping to what Nicole assumed was a rerun of Lyla Dane's plea for her daughter's safe return, but she was numb.

Before she could think what to do next, the doorbell rang. Startled by the unexpected sound, she shakily swiped at the tears and took a step forward. She didn't feel the glass shards piercing her feet until she took the second step. At that point, sharp pains shot through her foot. She gasped, then looked down in confusion. Her legs looked as if she'd been running through mud, and she was standing in broken glass and ice cream, while a thin ribbon of blood seeped out from beneath her toes.

"Oh, no," Nicole mumbled, then stifled a second moan of pain.

The doorbell rang again. She shivered, then clutched her head in confusion.

"Just a minute!" she yelled, then tried to sidestep the rest of the debris as she hobbled to the door.

When she looked through the peephole in the door, she didn't know whether to be relieved or regretful.

It was Dominic, and as usual, she was a mess.

Nicole smiled a little self-consciously as she opened the door to let him in. "I just don't know what's happening to me. I think I'm losing my mind."

"Hey, don't talk about my woman like that."

Nicole rode the surge of delight his words brought. "So I'm still your woman?"

Dominic lowered his head.

Their lips met.

The kiss proceeded.

Slowly.

Thoroughly.

* * * * *

Be sure to look for the
AFTERSHOCK *anthology next month,*
as well as other exciting paranormal stories
from Silhouette Nocturne.
Available in October wherever books are sold.

nocturne™

SPECIAL EDITION™

FROM *NEW YORK TIMES* BESTSELLING AUTHOR

LINDA LAEL MILLER

A STONE CREEK CHRISTMAS

Veterinarian Olivia O'Ballivan finds the animals
in Stone Creek playing Cupid between her and
Tanner Quinn. Even Tanner's daughter, Sophie,
is eager to play matchmaker. With everyone
conspiring against them and the holiday season
fast approaching, Tanner and Olivia may just get
everything they want for Christmas after all!

*Available December 2008
wherever books are sold.*

REQUEST YOUR FREE BOOKS!

2 FREE NOVELS PLUS 2 FREE GIFTS!

HARLEQUIN®

Blaze™

Red-hot reads!

Silhouette® Romantic SUSPENSE

Sparked by Danger, Fueled by Passion.

USA TODAY bestselling author

Merline Lovelace

Undercover Wife

CODENAME: DANGER

Secret agent Mike Callahan, code name Hawkeye,
objects when he's paired with sophisticated
Gillian Ridgeway on a dangerous spy mission
to Hong Kong. Gillian has secretly been in love
with him for years, but Hawk is an overprotective
man with a wounded past that threatens to
resurface. Now the two must put their lives—
and hearts—at risk for each other.

Available October wherever books are sold.

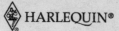

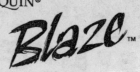

COMING NEXT MONTH

#423 LETHAL EXPOSURE Lori Wilde
Perfect Anatomy, Bk. 3
Wanting to expand her sexual IQ, Julie DeMarco selects Sebastian Black—hotshot PR exec—to participate in a no-strings fling. The playboy should be an easygoing love-'em-and-leave-'em type, but what if there's more to the man than just his good looks?

#424 MS. MATCH Jo Leigh
The Wrong Bed
Oops! It's the wrong sister! Paul Bennet agrees to take plain Jane Gwen Christopher on a charity date only to score points with her gorgeous sister. So what is he thinking when he wakes up beside Gwen the very next morning?

#425 AMOROUS LIAISONS Sarah Mayberry
Lust in Translation
Max Laurent thought he was over his attraction to Maddy Green. But when she shows up on the doorstep of his Paris flat, it turns out the lust never went away. He's determined to stay silent so as not to ruin their friendship—until the night she seduces him, that is.

#426 GOOD TO THE LAST BITE Crystal Green
Vampire Edward Marburn has only one goal left—to take vengeance on Gisele, the female vamp who'd stolen his humanity. Before long, Edward has Gisele right where he wants her. And he learns that the joys of sexual revenge can last an eternity....

#427 HER SECRET TREASURE Cindi Myers
Adam Carroway never thought he'd agree to work with Sandra Newman. Hit the sheets with her...absolutely. But work together? Still, his expedition needs the publicity her TV show will bring. Besides, what could be sexier than working out their differences in bed?

#428 WATCH AND LEARN Stephanie Bond
Sex for Beginners, Bk. 1
When recently divorced Gemma Jacobs receives a letter she'd written to herself ten years ago in college, she never guesses the contents will inspire her to take charge of her sexuality, to unleash her forbidden exhibitionist tendencies...and to seduce her totally hot, voyeuristic new neighbor....